THE DINNER PARTY

Also by Brenda Janowitz

THE DINNER PARTY

A NOVEL

Brenda Janowitz

ST. MARTIN'S GRIFFIN ❧ NEW YORK

THE DINNER PARTY. Copyright © 2016 by Brenda Janowitz. All rights reserved. Printed in the United States of America. For information, address St. Martin's Press, 175 Fifth Avenue, New York, N.Y. 10010.

www.stmartins.com

Designed by Omar Chapa

The Library of Congress Cataloging-in-Publication Data is available upon request.

ISBN 978-1-250-00787-2 (trade paperback)
ISBN 978-1-250-09556-5 (e-book)

Our books may be purchased in bulk for promotional, educational, or business use. Please contact your local bookseller or the Macmillan Corporate and Premium Sales Department at 1-800-221-7945, extension 5442, or by e-mail at Macmillan SpecialMarkets@macmillan.com.

First Edition: April 2016

10 9 8 7 6 5 4 3 2 1

To Doug, Ben, and Davey

BOOK ONE

The Seder Plate Is Assembled

The first question:
Why is this night different from all other nights?
On all other nights we eat leavened bread and matzoh,
but on this night only matzoh.

One

This Passover Seder is not just any Passover Seder. Yes, there will be a quick service followed by a festive meal, but this night is different from all other nights. This will be the night that the Golds of Greenwich meet the Rothschilds of New York City.

You may know the Rothschilds as the most famous Jewish family that ever lived. You may know them as the people who control banking. (When people say the Jews control banking, they are almost always talking about the Rothschilds.) And the Rothschilds have, for the last two hundred years, controlled banking in this country. They also own vineyards in Napa, diamond mines in Africa, and an organic farm somewhere in the Midwest that produces the most popular romaine lettuce consumed in this country.

The Rothschilds are the stuff of legends. Hollywood has made movies about them; historians have attempted to write books about them. And now, Sylvia's daughter is dating one of them.

Sylvia began planning for this Seder a month ago, when she discovered that her youngest of three had a new beau and planned to bring him. Sylvia was pleased that even during the insanity of medical school, Becca had made time for a social life. (Her middle child, Sarah, had no social life and an inappropriate beau.) Sylvia's pulse quickened when she discovered that her daughter's new boyfriend was a Rothschild. When Becca asked if his parents could attend the Seder, too, Sylvia all but fainted.

The first thing Sylvia did was have the gutters emptied. It was something she'd been planning to do (something she planned to do after every winter), but this time she actually did it. She couldn't risk any stray leaves falling on a Rothschild.

Next, she had the painter come in to freshen things up. Sylvia pointed out tiny cracks in the molding, little dings in the walls. She had the kitchen and powder room repainted. A fresh coat of paint on the front door.

Sylvia arranged to have a cleaning crew come to dry-clean the draperies. She had the rugs professionally cleaned, the wood floors refinished, the marble polished and resealed. A florist was commissioned to create a piece for the entryway table. ("The importance of a first impression cannot be overstated," the florist advised. Sylvia couldn't help but agree.)

Her husband had come home in the middle of all this. "How much is this Seder costing me, exactly?" he asked.

Alan didn't understand.

Sylvia wanted to present her home, her family, in a certain way. She looked at the house differently now that the Rothschilds were coming. She was very good at taking care of her home, but now she could only see what was wrong with it. Where before she saw in Becca's baby blanket, tenderly strewn across her childhood bed, a beautiful reminder of a time long past, now it was a remnant, threadbare and worn. The piano where Gideon learned to play, which she had always regarded as evidence of his happy childhood, was a rickety artifact in need of tuning. Sarah's old artwork, lovingly tacked to the back of her bedroom door, was childish and out of place.

Sylvia examined the guest bathroom with a diligent eye. Those towels on the wall—how long had she had them? She couldn't recall. They would need to be replaced. She made a trip into Manhattan to pick up new bath towels: white linen with a subtle silver pattern and a monogram. She also bought guest napkins and cocktail napkins for the bar in the same pattern.

She went back a week later when she decided that her tablecloth, the one she inherited from her Aunt Miriam, simply wouldn't do.

Four nights before her guests were to arrive, Sylvia set the table. She polished her old set of silver, the set she hadn't used since her mother was alive. It positively gleamed against the newly purchased napkins. Her old set of china—the set that was a wedding gift from Alan's parents—still looked modern and fresh. She would wait until the day of the Seder to buy fresh flowers for the table. She would arrange them in tiny vessels—five luscious red roses in each small vase—and place them all along the inside of the table. Everyone would have a view of the flowers, but they wouldn't be so high that you couldn't see the person sitting across from you. Sylvia imagined her finished table and silently complimented herself on her good taste. She'd always had an eye for the finer things.

Alan came downstairs to see when Sylvia was planning to turn in for the night.

"The table looks beautiful," he said. "What about the Seder plate?"

She had completely forgotten.

Two

"Do you have a shank bone?"

"No," Sarah replied. That's not exactly the sort of thing you keep around the kitchen. "Aren't you getting one from Marty?" Her mother had gone to the same butcher for as long as Sarah could remember. Had she had a falling-out with him? (Sylvia was prone to falling out with people who didn't meet her exacting standards.)

"I'm not," her mother said. "Can you get a shank bone, please?"

"I'm just going to walk in carrying a shank bone?"

The answer was yes, she should just walk in carrying a shank bone. Sarah hung up before realizing she hadn't asked about Marty. She had vivid memories of visiting his shop when she was a child. Her mother would pick her up from school, and on Mondays, Wednesdays, and Fridays, they'd drive to Goldsmith and Sons Kosher Butcher. Marty had a kind face, an unfortunate hairline, and a protruding gut—he looked like the image you would conjure when thinking of the word *butcher*. Marty always had a snack ready for Sarah. A meatball, a piece of turkey, the odd lollipop. He would smile broadly at her when she walked in. His shop always smelled like slow-roasted brisket.

Sarah puzzled over where, exactly, to purchase a shank bone, and when, exactly, to find the time to pick it up. It was Tuesday, and the Passover Seder was on Friday. She had a busy week of work ahead of her—the magazine went to print on Friday—and she would be going to the Seder straight from work once the issue went to bed.

"Can you pick up a shank bone this week?"

"And hello to you, too," Joe said.

"Sorry, honey," she said. "My mother is driving me crazy. She wants me to bring a shank bone. It's part of the Seder plate."

"I know that," he said. Of course he did. He'd been attending Gold family Seders since he was thirteen. Also, he'd been studying. "It represents the lamb that was the Paschal sacrifice on the eve of the exodus from Egypt."

"It does?" Sarah asked.

"Yes," Joe said. Sarah considered his response.

"Sorry," she said. "I know you know. She's driving me crazy."

"I noticed."

Joe knew that the Jewish holidays had a way of accentuating the fact that Sarah had chosen a Christmas-celebrating, Easter-observing Italian boy to spend her life with, and not the Hebrew-reading, Bar Mitzvah'd mensch that her mother had always hoped for. "Go back to work and I'll take care of everything."

"What are you wearing?"

"Dirty talk at the office?" Joe asked, his cheeks turning a slight shade of pink. "Okay, I'm down with that. I've got on my old Levi's—"

"I mean to the Seder," Sarah said.

"It's only Tuesday," he said.

"Exactly."

"How am I supposed to know what I'm wearing on Friday? It's only Tuesday."

"I'm wearing my gray shift—you know the one we did in the February issue?—with black tights and my black Loubie booties. Silver bangles, no necklace. Hair down."

She was doing it again. Talking in code. Speaking in that fashion editor's language that Joe could barely understand. But it didn't matter. Whatever Sarah draped herself in, Joe always thought she looked like she stepped off the pages of the magazine she edited.

"That sounds perfect," Joe said. This was usually the correct response.

"So, what are you going to wear? Those khakis I bought you?"

"I'm not really a khakis kind of guy."

"They would look really nice with the navy sports jacket I got you, and the tie I got you for the wedding."

"I'm not really a sports jacket kind of guy. I will shave, though."

"I'll pick something out for you," Sarah said, just before hanging up the phone.

Three

Sylvia loved wielding a knife. Loved the feel of it in her hands, the way it sliced through even the toughest foe with precision and speed.

A distant cousin had bought Sylvia her first set of knives as a wedding present. At the time, Sylvia thought it was a ridiculous gift. An offensive gift. After all, she was a nurse. She had a career. She felt that this present—most of the presents, actually—were objects meant to distract her from her goals and lure her into a more domesticated life. She certainly wasn't going to stop working just because she was getting married. Surely everyone understood that?

But soon after having the kids, Sylvia discovered the meditative power of cooking. Of slicing, in particular. And she cooked. Often. At first with recipes from her mother and her grandmother, and then by experimenting on her own. Sylvia discovered she was good in the kitchen. Very good. And Sylvia liked things at which she could excel.

Since then, Sylvia had graduated to more and more expensive sets of knives. She also owned her own sharpener, so she could treat her knives whenever they dulled. Sylvia did not like a dull knife.

Sylvia's kitchen was her sanctuary, her favorite room in the house. She had a large country kitchen before it was fashionable to do so. An oversized farmhouse sink, a large glass-front refrigerator, and an industrial double oven with eight burners and a griddle. The millwork was impeccable, the cabinets were double-glazed, and the countertops were granite. The edge of the kitchen island had a built-in butcher's block large enough to accommodate a Thanksgiving turkey.

Sylvia had insisted on a kitchen table that would seat ten. Alan objected—when hosting that many people, shouldn't we use the dining room?—but Sylvia got what she wanted, always got what she wanted, and liked to gloat whenever the table came in handy. Gideon's entire soccer team ate a victory pizza dinner at that table after winning regionals his junior year of high school. Becca's science club had created a large-scale replica of Mount Vesuvius when she was in the seventh grade. And Sarah's first-grade class took turns jumping onto the table and tracing their little selves for their unit on "The Human Body."

Sylvia stood at the kitchen island and cut up lemons for the chicken piccata. Alan loved to eat Italian right before Passover. The chicken encrusted in flour, the bed of pasta, the garlic toast on the side—exactly what he needed to get through eight days without bread. She looked out the bay window as she worked. How many times had she looked out that window while she was cooking to find her children running around the backyard? It was different now, with her son and daughters all grown up. No one really came home to visit anymore, except on holidays.

Sylvia looked back down at the cutting board. The lemon was cut into eight perfect circles. But there was something else on the board—a ribbon of deep burgundy all over her slices. Sylvia put down her knife and picked up the lemon slices to try to salvage them. Had they been ruined? Or could she bring them to the sink to rinse them off? As she picked up the fruit, she felt a searing sting on her hand—the pain was unbearable.

Sylvia had cut her finger.

Four

WISH YOU WERE HERE.

Sarah clicked "send" and her e-mail was whisked off her computer screen. Two nights before the holiday, and already she missed Gideon. She hated this feeling—no matter how angry she got at Gideon, no matter how much she hated him, he was, and always would be, her big brother. There was this longing, this need, to have him in her life. Even though when he was around, they fought more than anything else. Even though when he was around, Sarah became invisible.

Sarah flipped through the pages her assistant had dropped on her desk. Her changes hadn't been made. Did anyone here listen to her? She buzzed her assistant and instructed her to print out her changes (again) and send them to the art department (again).

"With a note explaining that we're resending the original edits?" her assistant asked.

"No note," Sarah said. "Just attach my original memo. The one they didn't follow."

Minutes later, an e-mail popped up on her screen: MISS YOU, TOO, KIDDO.

THE SEDER WON'T BE THE SAME WITH-
OUT YOU, she wrote. And then, as an afterthought: HOW
CAN YOU LEAVE ME ALONE WITH MOM?

Gideon quickly responded: ISN'T THAT WHAT JOE
IS FOR?

Sarah laughed and typed back: YES, BUT YOU ARE A
FAR BETTER DISTRACTION. HAVE TIME TO
SKYPE?

Sarah always forgot how to calculate the ten-and-a-half-hour
time difference between the East Coast and Sri Lanka.

A few clicks of the mouse, and her computer rang, inviting
Gideon Gold to a video chat. An enormous head popped up on
her screen.

"Don't they have razors over there?" she asked, staring at his
scruffy face.

"Hello to you, too," Gideon said, smiling broadly. He was
always smiling broadly. "I thought you missed me?"

"I'm just now realizing that I only want you for the distraction at the Seder."

"Gee, thanks, kiddo," he said. "Don't you know I'm doing
God's work over here?"

They both laughed. That was how Sylvia described Gideon's
job: doing God's work. Sarah liked to call Gideon "the Messiah,"
since that's how their mother treated him.

"What do you think of this new guy Becca's got?" Gideon
asked.

"I haven't met him yet," Sarah said.

"And he's coming to the Seder?"

"Well, he *is* a Rothschild," Sarah said.

"I have no idea what that means," Gideon responded, eyes bright, waiting for his sister's explanation.

Sarah was about to tell him about Becca's suitable boyfriend and his glamorous family when some sort of commotion flared up outside of Gideon's tent.

"Gotta go," he said, looking over his shoulder. "God's work just doesn't ever stop."

"Apparently not."

"I love you," he said, just as he ended the chat.

"I love you, too," she said to the blank screen.

Five

Sylvia left the most difficult thing until the end. She had a habit of doing that—leaving things she didn't want to do until the end. She'd done it before her wedding, deciding minutes before the ceremony who would walk with her in her father's absence. She'd done it before Gideon's Bar Mitzvah, deciding the day before who would light each of the thirteen candles on his cake. And she'd done it the year Sarah and Becca went away to college on the same day, deciding only two days before which parent would drive which girl.

She was doing it again now. The night before her guests were to arrive, Sylvia was finally tackling the seating arrangements. She knew the key to any successful dinner party was the placement of the guests.

She put each of the names on tiny little cards. There was her family: she and Alan, her daughters Sarah and Becca. As she wrote their names in her fanciest script, she couldn't help but feel a tug of emotion. Another year without Gideon. She knew that his work with Doctors Without Borders was important, but she hated the idea of him spending the holiday all alone, in a tent with no electricity.

Next she filled out the cards for Becca's boyfriend's family. There was the Boyfriend, Henry, and his parents, Ursella and Edmond. The Rothschilds. She wrote their names slowly, carefully, adding a flourish to her script on the *U* in Ursella's name and the *E* in Edmond's.

Finally, she brought herself to make out cards for Sarah's boyfriend and his mother. She wished that Sarah would break up with Joe. And she wished she hadn't been guilted into inviting his mother. (She'd only done so after the poor woman had a near-breakdown in the market on Front Street.) If anyone could ruin this dinner party, it was the Russos. Sylvia hastily wrote out cards for Joe and his mother. She wrote them so carelessly, in fact, that their names were barely legible. *Valentina* looked more like *Ballerina*, which she most certainly was not.

Next came the tiny sterling silver apples that would hold each place card. Sylvia started with the easiest ones. She and Alan would each occupy a seat at the head of the table, hers closer to the kitchen so she could check on the food as the meal progressed. Next, the Rothschilds. The Rothschilds should each have a seat of honor, so that was easy, too. Edmond would be seated to her right, Ursella to Alan's right, and Henry to her left. Once the guests of honor were placed, she stood back from the table to admire her handiwork.

Now came the hard part. Where would she put Joe's mother? Valentina had never been to their home before, but Sylvia knew that she'd be the most likely to cause a scene. She always spoke a decibel higher than most other people, like Stanley Kowalski yelling for Stella. And who knew what sorts of things she considered proper dinner conversation? She would put Valentina on

Alan's left. Surely he'd be able to manage her throughout the course of dinner. Alan had a way of speaking very softly. As a child, he was cautioned to be seen and not heard. And now, as the head of pediatric cardiology for Connecticut Children's Hospital, he was accustomed to people listening carefully to him. There was never an occasion to raise his voice; he always had the floor.

That left the girls and Joe. She put Becca next to her beau, and Sarah next to her. The only spot left for Joe was across the table from the girls, next to his mother. Maybe they would just talk amongst themselves.

Six

Spring in Manhattan was beautiful, truly beautiful. The snow boots went back in the closet, as did the winter coats and the mittens. The heavy sweaters, the bulky scarves, and the hats were no longer necessary. Out came the smart-looking raincoats and lightweight jackets. Suede shoes for the days it didn't rain. Compact umbrellas for the days it did.

Sarah loved the springtime. She loved that first day she could ditch her boots for a pretty pair of slingbacks. She loved being able to walk to work from the subway without all of the sidewalk sludge riding up on the backs of her calves. She loved the feel of the fresh air hitting her face after riding the train.

But once Sarah got to work, it was fall. The magazine worked six months ahead of time—every magazine did—so, even though it was spring in Manhattan, her mind was already on autumn. Back-to-school, fresh starts. New beginnings.

Sarah was very much in need of a new beginning. She loved reinventing herself. It was what had drawn her to the magazine world in the first place. Every season was another chance to change your wardrobe, change how the world saw you and how you saw yourself. She reveled in it.

Six months prior, Sarah had made a change. A big change. Like a snake that had shed its skin, she was a completely new being. Only most people didn't know it yet. Part of her liked it—this holding of an important secret—but part of her did not. Some days she felt as though the weight of it would crush her.

Sarah wanted to tell her mother. Really she did. But she couldn't. Not just yet. She had no idea how, for one thing. Or when.

"You and Joe will be on time?" her mother asked, seemingly for the millionth time.

"Yes," Sarah said. "We will be on time." She'd had no idea that she and Joe had cultivated such a reputation for lateness.

"Maybe even a few minutes early," her mother said. "Just so that the house is full when the Rothschilds arrive."

Sarah didn't respond; her assistant was dropping more pages onto her desk for approval. They were about to close August, and Sarah was in the all-important stage of reviewing final pages before they could go to print. She couldn't allow even the slightest error to make it through to the final book.

Sarah's desk was a mess. She hated a mess. Sarah liked order. She liked to know where things belonged. The rest of her office was perfectly organized—color-coded folders filled her filing cabinets, two startlingly white leather Barcelona chairs faced her desk, and her bookshelf held past issues of the magazine, stacked neatly, along with some of her own original artwork, all framed lovingly by Joe. Her windowsills were clear, save for a few picture frames, staged on top of hardcover books, chosen in equal parts for the meaningfulness of their titles (*The Best of Good* and *Time of My Life*) and the colors of their book jackets (pale pinks, light yellows). A small crystal vase sat on a table between the Barcelona chairs, filled with pink champagne peonies. Joe knew they were Sarah's favorite, and sent a bouquet each month the week the issue went to bed.

"Did you hear me?" Sylvia asked.

"Yes," Sarah said, on autopilot, as she flipped through the draft pages. "Be on time."

"Be early," Sylvia said.

"I always am," she said.

Sarah snuck out of her office for lunch. She couldn't recall the last time she'd done that—taken a proper lunch break—and it made her feel like she was doing something illicit.

She couldn't decide if she liked that feeling or not.

Sarah walked down to the magazine's cafeteria (she wasn't so bold as to actually leave the building), and marveled at how many choices were on offer. When was the last time she'd been down here? Certainly when she was an intern and part of her job description was taking lunch orders, she'd spent half her day there. But had she been in the cafeteria in the last year or so? Sarah perused the choices: a salad bar with three types of greens (field mix, romaine, spinach), and a wide range of seeds (flax, chia, hemp); a panini station where hot sandwiches were made to order. She decided on a panini with grilled chicken and pesto, hold the cheese. Soon it would be Passover, which meant no bread for a week. It was a good idea to load up on carbs.

Sarah paid for her order and then walked into the dining room. As she saw tables filled with various editors and assistants, photographers and graphic artists, she realized that she had no one to sit with. She should have made plans before coming downstairs. It was like high school all over again.

She walked by a table with three girls from the art department. Shouldn't they be working on the pages she'd sent back? In fact, shouldn't all of these people be working right now? The issue was closing on Friday.

Sarah's tray rattled along, her pink lemonade threatening to spill with each step she took. Why couldn't she find a table filled with people she knew? People she liked? Sarah had friends at the magazine.

Didn't she?

She walked the full circle of the dining room, and then headed back up to her office to eat lunch at her desk.

Seven

It was a tiny little hair. One gray hair in the midst of many long blond ones. Becca stared at it for a long time. These tiny little gray hairs were appearing with more frequency lately; Becca was shocked every time she discovered a new one. Can a twenty-two-year-old even get a gray hair? She twisted and turned the strand of hair, pretending she wasn't going to pull it out. She knew that she would.

It had become ritual, a part of her morning routine. She'd discovered the first one when she was blow-drying her hair straight one day. Her hair was divided into sections, ready to be forced into submission, when Becca noticed a wayward strand sticking out sideways from her head. She brushed it down with her hand, only to have it pop right back out. It seemed to defy the rules of gravity; she couldn't get this one to lie down with the rest of the hairs on her head. She got closer to the mirror, curious to examine this strand of hair that challenged the rules of nature. But it was not a regular hair at all.

For one thing, it had a different consistency. She had a long, thick mane of silky locks, but this one was short and wiry. This one was tough. Without really thinking about it, she pulled the hair out, right at the root. It was then that she noticed its hue. It wasn't coppery, or buttery, or even caramel.

It was silver.

The next day, she began looking for more. It became a game—how many gray hairs could she pull out on any given day? She'd stand in front of the mirror, flipping her head this way and that, hoping to section her hair off in just the right spot so as to find another offender.

Usually she stuck with the hairs close to the base of her neck or in the middle of her head, the ones you wouldn't notice were gone. But this little hair had a lot of nerve, showing up in her part, just at her hairline, where everyone would see it. Becca pulled the hair out, and with it, three other non-gray hairs. It startled her slightly to see that she'd pulled so much hair from the front of her head, but when looked at herself in the mirror she decided that it wasn't noticeable. She went on with her makeup routine. When her thoughts floated to this evening's Seder, she tossed her hair to the side to look for some more.

Becca was good at everything. Except sitting still. She was always doing, thinking, accomplishing. She didn't know how to do it any other way.

Her college boyfriend once asked her why she always felt like she had to be doing something. But Becca didn't understand the question. Didn't everyone feel this way? There were endless amounts of things to do: applications to complete, closets to be organized, opportunities to seek out. How could she spend a

Saturday afternoon just sitting around when there were so many things on her to-do list?

Complete schoolwork, go to internship, apply for residency, hold teaching assistant office hours, read the newspaper, read medical journals, read a book, go to the supermarket, go to the dry cleaners, go to the drugstore, send out birthday cards, send out holiday cards, buy presents, buy presents, buy presents, put photographs into albums, call mother, call father, call sister, call brother, go to the doctor, go to the dentist, go to the ob-gyn, attend cooking class with the girls, attend movie night with the friends, go shopping with the mother, get yearly shots, get haircut. Repeat.

Becca was very busy.

And she was very good.

In the second grade, Becca's teacher had encouraged her to enter a storytelling competition. There were whispers about how seriously Becca took her studies, even back then, and her teacher thought that this might be a good way for her to enjoy an extracurricular activity. To have fun learning, she told her mother. Sylvia objected at first. Weren't her daughter's grades the best in the class? Becca's teacher confirmed that yes, Becca was her best student, but she wanted her to enjoy it a little bit more. Sylvia relented and let Becca enter the competition. After all, she knew that her daughter would win.

Students were to memorize a book, and then re-tell the story to an audience. Points were awarded for remembering the story word for word, but also for presentation. In fact, more points would be given to the student who presented the story in the most dynamic way. Becca practiced for days on end, her mother as her doting audience. With each read through, Sylvia would sit with the book in her lap, grinning from ear to ear as her daughter recalled each word perfectly. Becca would memorize the book flawlessly. There was never any doubt.

The big day came. Becca wore the new outfit her mother had bought especially for the competition: a navy dress with a flared skirt, trimmed with white piping. Becca felt very adult. For one thing, the dress was very mature-looking. Also, her mother had bought her a brand-new pair of shoes with a tiny platform. They weren't heels, exactly, but they gently raised the pitch of her foot half an inch so she felt like she was tiptoeing around. The outfit referenced a nautical theme (but it wasn't a sailor suit—that would be too on-the-nose, Sylvia felt), in keeping with the book Becca had memorized: *Sally's Adventure at Sea*.

Becca was set to present last. As she watched her competition from backstage, she recognized a familiar feeling setting in. One she felt at the start of any academic challenge: *I am going to win.* She watched the first boy fumble his lines and then tear up. The second contestant, a girl with a cumbersome back brace, was counting on her cuteness to get her by. Becca could tell that she wasn't repeating the book word for word—more like her own interpretation of it. *That's not what the contest is*, she thought. Then, it was Becca's turn. She knew her story backward and forward. There was no way this contest wasn't hers.

But it wasn't. The girl with the back brace won. Apparently her "dramatic flair" was the thing that clinched it for her. The judges commended her understanding of the material, and her innate storytelling abilities. As they left the auditorium, Becca's mother whispered into her ear that the only reason they had given it to that other girl was because of her back brace.

Becca thought about the competition from time to time. The one blemish on an otherwise perfect academic record. In fact, she wrote one of her college applications about it: "The Merits of Failing," she called it. To her, it was a lesson. You must always try harder.

Eight

Sylvia crashed into Alan as she rushed through the master bedroom.

"Get out of my way! Don't you know what an important night this is for me?"

"I know, Syl. I know. What I don't get is why you care so much what these people think of us," Alan said. "Becca and Henry have only been dating for three months."

"Do you know who this boy is?" she asked. "Who his father is?"

"I think that my daughter should be dating a man, not a boy."

Sylvia furrowed her brow. She hated when Alan got pedantic. "You know what I mean."

"I'm not sure I do," he said. "Slow down."

"I can't slow down!" Sylvia cried. "Our guests will be here in an hour!"

Alan was already dressed—and not in the outfit she'd laid out for him. He had on gray trousers, a light-yellow dress shirt, and a baby-blue cashmere cardigan. He looked like Mr. Rogers. Still, Sylvia had no time to think about what her husband was wearing. She had to get herself dressed. The outfit she'd laid out for herself, planned out for herself weeks earlier, now looked suburban. Dowdy, even.

"Should I wear a St. John suit?" she called to Alan from the depths of her walk-in closet. "She wears a lot of St. John suits."

"How do you know what Henry's mother wears?" Alan asked, appearing at her closet door. Sylvia grabbed a nearby bathrobe and covered herself.

"I Googled her," she said quietly. She wasn't exactly embarrassed about admitting this, but she wasn't proud of it, either. Alan could tell because she wasn't looking him in the eye. Sylvia always looked him directly in the eye.

In Alan's experience, Googling anything was a bad idea. Patients routinely came into his office demanding a tilt test, or an EKG, or any other of the myriad things they'd gleaned from WebMD before coming to his office. He had once caught Becca in his office Googling an ex-boyfriend when she was supposed to. be shadowing a pediatric cardiology resident.

"I don't think Googling this boy's parents is a good idea," he said gently.

"Is it so bad that I worry about my daughter?" she asked, pushing Alan out of her closet and shutting the door behind him.

"How come you never worry about Gideon?" Alan asked the closet door.

Sylvia walked out. She was wearing a skirt suit.

"You look like you're off to *shul*," he said.

"What's wrong with dressing up for a holiday?"

"Nothing," he said. "But I think you'd do better in pants and no heels. You need to be comfortable if you're going to be the hostess."

"Life is harder for a woman," Sylvia said, and retreated to her closet.

Alan wasn't sure if she was talking about what to wear to the Seder or his previous question—why she never worried about Gideon.

Nine

Sarah opened her jewelry box—a large wooden box painted a faint white and lined in red velvet. The same jewelry box she'd had as a little girl. The same jewelry box she'd brought to college, and then to her first apartment in the city. And now to the home she shared with Joe. She ran her fingers over its contents—large, chunky designer pieces, some gifts from the designers themselves, some taken from photo shoots (not stolen, just permanently borrowed), and some gifted to her by other editors at holiday time. Old gold heart earrings, a gift from her parents for her sixteenth birthday; a gold ring with the Hebrew word *Chai* that her grandmother had bought her for her Bat Mitzvah; a stainless steel bracelet watch engraved with the words: CONGRATULATIONS ON YOUR GRADUATION. LOVE, MOM AND DAD.

Then, the things that Joe had bought her over the years. A pair of jade earrings purchased in Las Vegas when Joe was at a bachelor party and had a run of luck at the craps table. A delicate silver ring that he'd given her shortly before their senior prom, all he could afford on his part-time salary from his father's gas station. A gold necklace with a charm that read LOVE that Sarah had worn all throughout college, even during the periods when she and Joe weren't an item.

Sarah lifted the tray to reveal another section of the jewelry box, the hidden section, with the jewelry she couldn't wear. Wouldn't wear. But still, she liked to visit it every so often.

Sarah chose two chunky silver bangles and slid them onto her wrist. She noticed that her nail polish—a dark navy that her magazine, Sarah really, had proclaimed the "it" shade for spring— had a tiny chip on the index finger. She licked the edge of her finger, as if to fix it.

She turned toward the mirror to see how the bangles looked with her dress. *Those aren't the real you.* She could hear her mother's voice in her head. Her mother felt that the spoils of her fashion career didn't reflect the real Sarah. Sarah's mother wanted her to wear the jewelry that meant something, the pieces that had been given to her by her family. Pieces that were significant, that marked some milestone or had belonged to someone important. But Sarah couldn't very well wear a pair of earrings in the shape of hearts any more than she could wear a flannel shirt tied around her waist.

Sarah modeled the bracelets, turning this way and that, examining every square inch of her appearance. The gray shift was body-conscious, but not vulgar. The hemline was the perfect length—courtesy of the in-house tailors the magazine employed— and the booties gave the look some much-needed edge. The bangles added interest to an otherwise plain sheath. Sarah was pleased with how she looked. If she really thought about it, she'd find it amusing that she'd chosen a career where outward appearance was so important, being that she had been teased mercilessly as a child for her appearance.

But she didn't really think about it.

Ten

Alan sat in his study, reading the paper. There was a time when he would help his wife get ready for guests, but he's learned that the house is Sylvia's, he just gets to live here.

Which is fine by him. Sylvia decorated his study to be warm and inviting, a place where he could take his coffee and read through the newspaper or his medical journals without being disturbed. The walls were lined with mahogany bookshelves, hand carved and stained. Medical journals filled the shelves, as did family photographs in sterling silver frames, sports memorabilia. A baseball signed by Sandy Koufax sat in a case next to one with a Super Bowl ticket (all he had with him at the time!) signed by Joe Namath. A Lladró statue of a doctor, a graduation gift from his parents, sat atop his medical school yearbook. The back walls of the bookshelves were painted a deep red—years before it was popular, Sylvia would hasten to add. The mahogany wainscoting on the ceiling finished the look, making it seem like it had always looked like this.

Alan scanned the business pages of the *Times*. He wouldn't Google the Rothschilds—that he wouldn't do—but there was nothing wrong with brushing up on what was happening in the financial world.

The house Alan lives in now is far different than the house he grew up in. A home filled with two Holocaust survivors who feared going to the dentist and refused to stand on line. Parents who never slept at night. The house Sylvia made for them has a feeling of warmth. A feeling of comfort. His childhood home was cold. There had been no rugs on the floor; the furniture was sparse. Nothing adorning the walls. It was as if his parents wanted to be ready, if they ever needed to again, to run and hide.

Alan wasn't allowed to have friends over. "Who *are* those people?" his mother would ask. Alan's parents didn't trust anyone but other Holocaust survivors. They didn't entirely trust them, either. It was easy to avoid the outside world in their tiny Brooklyn enclave. His father worked as a haberdasher just blocks from their home. His mother rarely left the house. The only socializing they did was on holidays, and that was with other Holocaust survivors. People Alan barely knew. They had no family.

Alan was embarrassed by his parents. He was scared of them. He wanted very little to do with them.

Alan Gold met Sylvia Fischer when she was working at Connecticut Children's Hospital. Everything about her was an aberration. Most Jewish women worked as teachers in those days, or married well, so they wouldn't have to work. But Sylvia was a nurse. Not that Alan could tell she was Jewish with her Grace

Kelly hair, deep-blue eyes, and porcelain skin. Her maiden name was Fischer, which, in Alan's experience, could go either way.

But Sylvia didn't want to date Alan. She was there to work. Unlike the other nurses who batted their eyes as they reported on his patients and asked for his signature on paperwork, Sylvia was a model of efficiency. She was known as the best nurse in pediatric cardiology, and doctors fought to get her on their shifts.

The children themselves didn't love her, but their parents did. As the parents of a three-year-old surgery patient had explained to Alan, "When Sylvia tells you something, you know it's true."

Sylvia had always wanted to be a doctor. She took her studies seriously. "I sent you to college to find someone to marry," her mother would tell her. To which Sylvia would respond, "You didn't send me, I sent myself." She was right, of course; she'd earned a scholarship to school. But her mother worried. Sylvia was no great beauty, her one chance at finding someone was at college, where she could impress the young men with her intellect, of which she had plenty.

But Sylvia wanted more.

The first time Alan asked her out, she said no. That had never happened to Alan before and it made him laugh. As he watched her walk away from him, back to the nurses station, he wanted to yell: *You should see the women I usually date!* But he put his head into his patient's chart and slowly skulked away.

The second time he asked her out, he was sure she would say yes. They'd just come off a rough shift—twin babies delivered nine weeks early, both with major congenital heart disease, a five-year-old diagnosed with a condition that would necessitate a complicated surgery, and a nine-year-old with Down syndrome whose heart had simply given out. Alan decided to treat the staff to a late-night dinner. On him, of course. Everyone was delighted to accept the invitation. Everyone but Sylvia. As she explained her need to get some rest before her next shift started, he interrupted, saying: "It's not even a date! It's a bunch of co-workers blowing off some steam after a rough day!"

Sylvia was not fazed. She explained to Dr. Gold that yes, she did understand that, and no, she would not be able to attend. That night, even as the most junior nurse on staff—a sultry redhead with the face of Ann-Margret and the body of Marilyn Monroe—flirted shamelessly with him, all he could think about was Sylvia.

Eleven

The house felt empty now that Dominic was gone. Valentina could almost swear it had an echo.

She still cooked elaborate dinners each night, as if Dom were coming home to her. All of his favorites: veal Parmesan, baked manicotti, shrimp scampi. She didn't know how to cook for fewer than six; that's not how she'd been taught back in her grandmother's kitchen. Each night, she'd cook for hours, preparing a feast—salad, antipasto, homemade pasta, and a main course—and then eat her dinner quietly, alone, at the dining room table. Once she was done, she'd freeze the leftovers, certain she'd eat them another day. But she never did. And her freezer had run out of room.

Friends invited her over to eat—she had gone to her older sister's house four out of the five Sundays since Dominic had been gone—but it just wasn't the same. Valentina longed for Dominic's company. Those nights they'd linger over dinner. Dominic telling her she was beautiful, bringing her flowers for no reason. Every night, they would eat in the dining room, as if dinner were a grand occasion, and every night, Dominic would carry on about her food—how it was the best he had ever tasted.

The chicken, the most tender; the pasta, the freshest; the sauce, the sweetest. Even better than his mother used to make, rest her soul.

She still had red wine with dinner. (It's good for the heart, she told herself, when she worried about the type of woman who drank alone.) She savored every sip, every bite. She imagined that Dominic was still there, sitting catty-cornered to her, complimenting her at every turn. *These candlesticks are beautiful! No one sets a table like my Valentina! Even the neighbors can smell how delicious our kitchen is!*

Valentina had invited Sarah's mother over to eat countless times, but Sylvia always seemed to have something to do, somewhere she had to be, even during the Super Bowl parties that she and Dominic threw each year.

Valentina suspected that Sylvia didn't like her very much, which was why she was surprised to even be invited to this dinner party. And a Jewish holiday, to boot! She suspected it had something to do with her breakdown in the frozen foods aisle. But Dominic loved pigs in a blanket—he thought they really classed up a party—and seeing that party pack of Nathan's had just really sent her over the edge.

Twelve

"What are you wearing tonight?" Sarah asked.

"Pants and a shirt, why?" Alan knew that his answer would not satisfy his daughter, but he could never figure out exactly what made one pair of slacks different from the other.

Still, he loved to give her a hard time.

"What are *you* wearing?" Alan asked.

"I just need to know what to put Joe in," she said.

"What to put him in? Joe is a grown man," he said. "I think he probably knows how to dress himself."

Joe did not know how to dress himself. Beyond his usual uniform of jeans and a work shirt, Joe had no idea how to put an outfit together. He never met an occasion that he felt jeans would be inappropriate for.

Sarah was partially at fault for this. She'd been picking out his clothes ever since he first let her, for the seventh grade homecoming dance, when they'd agreed to a coordinating teal tie to match Sarah's dress. He never had to give clothing much thought. Even an ill-fated subscription to a men's fashion magazine was no help. Joe never read it, thinking Sarah had gotten it for herself—something about sussing out the competition.

"If I let him dress himself, he'd come to the Seder wearing jeans," Sarah said, with something like a guffaw escaping her lips.

"Would that be so bad?" Alan asked. "Maybe it would be nice to have a more casual holiday one of these years. Tell you what—if Joe wants to wear jeans, I will, too."

Sarah laughed to herself. She could just see it now: Sylvia's guests, marching to the door in a sea of jeans and untucked shirts, like a zombie apocalypse.

Sarah remembered the holidays of her childhood. Blouses with lace trim on the edges, thick tights, dresses that looked like miniature versions of what her mother would wear. And high heels. Sylvia would always let her girls wear shoes with a tiny heel for the holidays. It made Sarah feel so grown up. She lived for the times she could wear her dressy shoes. They made her feel adult. They made her feel important.

"Do you even *own* jeans?" Sarah asked her father.

"As a matter of fact, I do," Alan replied. "Very hip ones, I might add."

"It's a holiday," Sarah said. "I'm sure that Mom has told you that we're expected to dress up."

"No," Alan said. "In fact, your mother didn't mention anything like that to me at all. Was there a dress code for tonight?"

They both laughed, possibly a little too much.

"Wear a tie," she said, and Alan could swear he was talking to Sylvia.

"I'm not wearing a tie," he said, patting down his outfit. "I have on a cardigan."

"A cardigan?" Sarah asked, exasperated. *A cardigan?* "I'm making Joe wear a tie. Please put on a tie."

"Yes, dear," Alan said. And with that, he went back upstairs to add a tie to what he considered to already be a very smart ensemble.

Thirteen

Henry was not the smartest person in his family, but he was determined to show that he was. He just didn't want to work too hard at it.

It never dawned on him that once he left the golden cage of the Upper East Side life would be different. He still expected to lead the same life he'd led up until that point—a life filled with domestics, women who lusted after him, and everything he ever wanted served up for him on a silver platter. He hadn't gotten into any of the colleges his father had handpicked for him. His grades from his third-tier Manhattan prep school were atrocious, and his SAT scores were even worse. His father had been counting on Henry's college application essay (which he had paid good money for) and his own connections to get Henry into Princeton, his alma mater. What did they think those enormous endowments were for, anyway? Dartmouth rejected him mere hours after receipt of the application, and Brown didn't even have the grace to send a rejection. They'd had to call to find out the bad news. Apparently, Henry's rejection letter was lost in the mail.

The University of Florida was the only school that would take him, and with him, a check for the new library they were looking to build. Henry's parents encouraged him to go, under the misguided notion that he would take college seriously, and that they could keep an eye on him from their winter hideaway in Palm Beach. It only took one semester for the University of Florida to send Henry packing. The dean called Henry's father personally to give him the news. It seemed Henry had not attended any classes in the one semester that he'd been there, and then had sent in another student to take his final exams for him. "We can forgive a lot," the dean explained in a conspiratorial tone, "but a blatant disregard for the Code of Conduct is not one of them." A few days later, the check Henry's father had sent for the library was mailed back to him, with a personal note of apology from the dean, thus restoring Edmond's faith in humanity, if not in his son.

It wasn't fair, Henry thought in the days after being sent home from Florida. How was he expected to survive in college when he'd been given so few tools to do so? It was like hurling a baby bird out of the nest before teaching it to fly.

Since coming home, he'd spent most of his time at Columbia's library. He wasn't studying—he was waiting for his friends from high school to come and study after their classes. Four of his friends had gone on to attend Columbia and he could usually convince at least one of them to blow off studying.

The bars by Columbia were amazing. Much better than the ones in Florida. They had clever names like The Library, The Dead Poet, and Hemingway's. The top bar at Florida was called The Swamp.

And the best part of these bars was that they were always filled, no matter what time of day. It was four o'clock on a Thursday when Henry met Becca. She was seated at the bar, and when her girlfriend left, Becca stayed back, nursing her pint of beer and order of fries. It was only when Henry sat down on the bar stool next to her that he realized she was crying.

"What does a pretty girl like you have to cry about?" Henry asked. It wasn't a line. He really couldn't believe that a girl like her, with her long mane of blond hair, crystal blue eyes, and lithe frame, would have anything to cry about. In his experience, girls who looked like that usually got what they wanted.

"Nothing," she said, looking into her beer. "Everything."

"It can't be that bad," he said. "Maybe you're done with the drinking for now." He motioned to the bartender to get her a cup of coffee.

She shook her head at the bartender. "A glass of vodka, please."

Henry laughed. "You don't drink straight vodka."

"How do you know what I do and don't drink?" she asked. Henry decided that the way her lips curled into a snarl was the cutest thing he had ever seen in his life.

"You just don't look like the type who day drinks," he said. "Here, I think a cup of coffee is what you need."

"I don't drink coffee."

"Who doesn't drink coffee?" he said. "I've never met someone who didn't drink coffee before. Wait, you aren't one of those tea drinkers, are you?"

"What?" she asked. "No. But is drinking tea bad?"

"Tea drinkers are a different breed. We coffee drinkers have to stick together."

She had no idea what he was talking about, but somehow,

he got her to laugh. She tried a sip of the coffee—it was bitter, so bitter—and put the cup back down on its saucer. It was the first sip of coffee Becca had ever had in her life. She never needed caffeine. Usually her nervous energy was enough to fuel a cruise ship. But she had been feeling tired lately. Exhausted, really. And she felt utterly, completely adrift. If she wasn't always running, always doing, who was she?

"I got the internship I applied for," she told Henry. Becca felt like she could tell her secrets to this stranger. After all, isn't someone you'll never see again the perfect person to confess to?

"That's great!" Henry said. "So, then, why are you crying?"

"Because I got the internship I applied for."

"You didn't want it?" he asked. Henry was confused. The girls he usually met in bars, even smart ones like Columbia bars, were easy. This girl seemed difficult.

"Yes, I did want it," she said. "I'm just so tired."

"Well, that's why I got you this coffee."

"It tastes disgusting."

"May I?" Henry asked. Becca nodded and he added sugar and cream to the cup. She took a sip and smiled.

"Mmm," she murmured.

The edges of Henry's mouth curled up. *Now, that's a sound I'd like to hear more often.*

"May I take you out for dinner tonight?" he asked.

Becca had her orientation for her internship that night. She knew people were depending on her. But she still said yes.

Fourteen

"Why aren't you ready?" Sarah trilled as Joe walked in the door. He hadn't expected her to be home so early. In fact, he hadn't expected her to be home at all. He thought she would meet him at the Seder, straight from the train. He'd hoped for a few minutes to relax after work, a quick beer (always a quick beer before dealing with Sarah's mother), and a hot shower to wash off the day.

"How do you know I'm not ready?" he asked.

Sarah responded with a look.

"What?" Joe asked, edging up to Sarah. "These jeans aren't appropriate for dinner at your family's house?"

Joe approached Sarah slowly. He had no intention of actually touching her (he knew that if he sullied her dress he would never hear the end of it), but he was getting a kick out of her reaction. Sarah had once casually mentioned to him that he "knew how to wear a pair of jeans," and that was something that Joe had never forgotten. Jeans had become his official uniform from that day forward.

"Don't touch me!" Sarah cried. "You're covered in grease!"

"You don't like my shirt?" he asked, taking it off. He stood in front of Sarah bare-chested, in a pair of jeans that he knew how to wear. They had over an hour until the Seder began. It only took Joe seven minutes to get showered and throw clothes on. The drive to Sarah's parents' house was only ten minutes, so if he played his cards right . . .

"You need to take a shower!" she said.

A shower sounded like an excellent idea. Joe arched his eyebrows, and tilted his head toward the shower. *Shower for two?*

"Are you insane?!" Sarah half whispered, half yelled. "Go get ready!"

Joe took less than ten minutes to shower, shave, and dress. In fact, he was coming out of the bedroom just as Sarah was giving him her twenty-minute warning.

"We're leaving in twen—" She stopped short. "What is that?" she asked.

"What's what?" he repeated, innocently, as if he didn't know what she was talking about. Sarah was waiting in the living room. Had she been standing here this entire time, waiting for him to get showered, shaved, and dressed?

"I thought I told you to wear the tie I got you for the wedding?"

"This is a tie substitute," Joe explained. He thought that someone who worked in fashion would know something like this.

"A what?" Sarah asked, a look of horror slowly registering on her face.

"A tie substitute," Joe said, positioning himself in front of the mirror so he could admire the strange piece of string dangling around his neck

"Well, you can't wear it."

"Well, I am wearing it." He turned to her and smiled.

Whenever Joe thinks he's losing an argument, he always flashes her a big smile.

He's always had a perfect smile. These are the types of things you know about a person you've known since you were thirteen years old. Just as Joe knows that Sarah's teeth are only perfect because of four very painful years of braces. And that the kids in middle school used to call her Bugs, because her gigantic overbite and two very large front teeth made her look like Bugs Bunny. Her teeth have been perfect for over ten years, but Sarah still doesn't ever show them to anybody.

"I really don't want you to wear that thing—"

"It's a lariat," he said.

"I don't care what you call it," she said, "you can't wear it to my parents' house."

"So, this is what this is all about," he said, as if he'd just figured it out now, for the very first time. "Your mother."

"This is not about my mother," Sarah said, her words clipped. "It's the first Passover Seder. You need to wear a tie."

"There's nothing in the Book of Exodus that says you need to wear a tie."

"Don't get cute with me."

"I can't help it," he said, and shrugged his shoulders. "I *am* cute."

Sarah knew there was only one solution. Just one way out. The only way to rectify this situation was to seduce him. To get him undressed and into bed. Then, in the afterglow, when they hurried to get re-dressed, she could casually suggest that he wear an actual tie. There would be no way for him to deny her.

In the sexiest way possible, she said: "You *are* cute," and then proceeded to unzip her dress and let it fall to the ground. She took the clip out of her hair, let the strands fall to her shoulders in a way that she thought would be considered beguiling, and gave Joe her best come hither look.

And he did. Come hither, that is. They kissed. She unbuttoned his shirt, his pants, quickly. Then Joe started laughing and pulled away.

"You know," he whispered into Sarah's ear, "we can have sex now, but I'm still going to wear the lariat."

She pushed him away and put her dress back on.

Fifteen

Sylvia imagined Ursella Rothschild walking into her home for the first time. Was the entryway pristine? Were the flowers standing at attention? Was the powder room spotless?

Well, hello!

Welcome to my home.

Welcome to our home, we're so pleased you could make it.

Sylvia examined the entryway wallpaper. One of the edges was peeling, ever so slightly. She chastised herself for not thinking to get it replaced. Wasn't grasscloth the latest trend? But then she imagined how taken Ursella would be with the floral arrangement Sylvia had commissioned for the entryway table, and her shoulders began to release.

May I take your coats?

Sylvia opened the front closet. She smiled as she saw that her hard work in staging was a success. The wood hangers, all in the same dark glaze, were lined up perfectly, all leaning in the same direction. The shelf above the hanging rod held two large wicker baskets, one overflowing with sports equipment, the other filled with gloves and scarves and hats. *We're an outdoorsy family*, it said. *You like to ski in Aspen? We love to ski, too!*

The smell of pine drifted out subtly. Sylvia had been very specific with the salesperson that the smell of the hangers should not be overpowering.

On to the powder room. The lavender soap bottle was almost full. She didn't want it to be completely full (like she was trying too hard), but she didn't want it to run out over the course of the dinner, either. The new linen hand towels were perfect, just perfect. She fingered the edge of one as she looked at herself in the mirror.

On to the dining room, where Sylvia went over the table settings. Again. Joe was seated next to Edmond. That was probably a mistake. What could Joe possibly have to talk about with Edmond Rothschild? Transmissions?

So Sarah and Joe were switched. This put Joe next to Ursella. Sylvia sighed. It would be easier to do the table arrangements without Joe. She took his tiny little place card and put it on the sideboard. She would worry about where to put him after she did her final run-through of the house. If only it were as easy to get rid of him in real life.

Sylvia knows times are different now. She knows you don't have to make a good marriage, like she had to when she was young. She doesn't want to pressure her daughter like her mother pressured her. Still, she thinks Sarah could do much, much better than Joe.

Being married to a smart, handsome, wealthy doctor certainly has worked out well for Sylvia. It may not have been her childhood dream, this life she was living, but it was a dream come true. There was no doubt about that.

Was it wrong to want the same for her daughters?

If she had her druthers, Sarah would be attending this dinner with a new, more appropriate boyfriend, and the table would be perfect. But she had created the best table she could, given the circumstances. She called for Alan to come downstairs, to admire her handiwork.

"Looks good," he said.

"You barely looked at it," she said.

"I looked at it," he said, with a laugh in his voice, "but anyway, I never have to worry. Everything you do is perfect."

She smiled. Somewhere deep inside of her, she hated that she needed Alan's approval on everything, but she shoved that feeling down, reveling in the fact that Alan thought it looked perfect.

Sylvia had never thought it would happen for her. A relationship, that is. She never thought she'd be able to find anyone who was in love with her, much less someone handsome and rich. Someone who had money, who would give her all the things she'd never had in her life. Who would make sure her mother never had to work or worry about money again.

Sylvia had been so proud to graduate college, even though most of her friends had left college already to get married. After she had collected her diploma, she rushed to her mother's side, sure that she had finally made her proud. But her mother didn't even look at the diploma. She tried to smile for her daughter's benefit, but Sylvia could see it in her eyes. Her mother wasn't happy that Sylvia had graduated—she was disappointed. As her mother calmly explained to her later that day, Sylvia was an old maid now. She had missed her window. She would never get married.

But, she did. And if she really thinks about it, it fills her with joy to know that her daughters can have the opportunities she never had. Becca was fulfilling Sylvia's life's dream by becoming a doctor. Sarah was diddling about in the fashion world, but Sylvia held out hope that she'd eventually come to realize she belonged in medical school. And on the arm of a more respectable beau.

Still, she sleeps with one eye open. Even after thirty years of marriage, she's still wary. Still thinks he's going to leave her. That's why she always works so hard, that's why she fights, fights, fights.

Sixteen

Ursella had wanted to ship Henry off to a military academy. This was way back when he first started getting failing grades, before it was too late. Ursella said Edmond coddled Henry. But Edmond saw no reason why his son couldn't benefit from all of the advantages he'd had as a boy. He'd had his father's help getting into Princeton. He had joined the family business upon graduation. There was no denying the old boy network—why shouldn't his son reap the benefits?

It took Edmond far too long to see what was happening. He made excuses.

He's just a boy.

It's only middle school.

He'll come out of it.

Ursella tried to change Edmond's mind, but Edmond wouldn't hear of it. He'd been shipped off to boarding school, and he resented it. He felt a child's place was with his parents, and did whatever he had to do to keep Henry enrolled in his Manhattan prep school.

Edmond's own father had spoken of character—the sort of character that could only be earned by attending a school two hundred and twenty-three miles from one's childhood home. Each fall, Edmond would beg his mother to let him stay home and attend a school in Manhattan, but each fall, his mother reminded Edmond of his responsibility to his family; after all, as the eldest of four siblings, it was incumbent on him to show the others what was best for all of them.

Edmond and Ursella fought often about Henry. Edmond felt that Ursella didn't spend enough time at home. She should be helping him with his schoolwork more, rather than focusing on her myriad charity commitments. Ursella felt that Edmond should spend fewer late nights at the office.

What could he do? There was something Edmond wasn't telling Ursella, something he'd kept from her for over a year. (But more on that later.)

The cheating scandal. Henry would never come back from that, Edmund decided. How could he?

This girl. This girl, with her impressive family and medical school background—she was the answer. She would set Henry straight. She would make him a better man.

Seventeen

Edmond emerged wearing his best gray pin-striped suit and a red silk tie patterned with tiny boats. "You look like you're running for office," Ursella said in her heavily accented English. Edmond had found her accent so sexy when they first met. He still did.

Ursella retreated to her walk-in closet. She dressed carefully as Edmond stood watching. She still had a dancer's body. Her back was muscular, taut, and lean. Her arms, still graceful and long. Muscle memory. She removed her silk kimono and stepped into the skirt of her suit. Slowly, she turned around. She felt his eyes on her. She could always feel his eyes on her.

"What are you looking at?" she asked.

"You," he said.

"You need to change your tie."

He dutifully went back to his closet and chose a pink silk tie, one with tiny elephants on it. By the time he got back to Ursella's closet, she was already dressed.

She wore a cream-colored knit skirt suit with delicate piping on the edges. Her high heels served to show off her legs. Ursella had great legs. Her hair was in the dancer's knot worn since forever. She wore very little makeup. When they first met, she routinely wore a dark crimson red lipstick that stained Edmond's face whenever he tried to kiss her. Which was often. Now, she wears a pale pink on her lips. But there don't seem to be many opportunities these days for stolen kisses.

"You look beautiful," he said. She didn't say thank you. She simply nodded. After all, it was a statement of fact.

Ursella examined her husband, every square inch of him— from the way he'd combed his hair, to the shave he'd gotten that afternoon at the barber, to his tie, to his socks.

"You look better."

Eighteen

"Wheels up in a half," Henry heard his father call from down the hall.

Henry hated being back in his childhood room. The corkboard that held up old photographs, mementos from his high school days, and invitations to the graduation parties he'd received. The navy-blue duvet that he'd been using since middle school. Even the embroidered pillow announcing his name and birth date seemed a painful reminder that he was too old to be living here.

His dorm room at college was smaller than his en suite bathroom at home, but still, he felt nostalgic for it. He even missed the shared bathrooms, filled with so much mold and filth you had to wear flip-flops to avoid getting a fungus infection. He thought about Becca's apartment. It was a tiny apartment, shared with three other girls, close to the Columbia campus, but it was hers. She might have only a 125-square-foot bedroom to call her own, but living there signaled freedom. It told the world that she was doing something with her life, she was going somewhere. She wasn't a fuck-up who'd cheated her way out of college.

His mother walked into his room without knocking, and marched toward his closet.

"You will wear this," she said, hanging a charcoal-gray suit on the door.

"Becca said I don't have to wear a suit," Henry said, his voice suddenly small. "I was going to wear my navy sports coat and a pair of gray pants."

"Let me see," Ursella said, and waited.

Henry motioned to his bed, where he'd laid out his clothes like a child.

"What tie?" she asked.

"I wasn't planning to wear a tie."

"You'll wear a tie," she said. "And the suit I've picked out. I want you to show some respect for this girl's family. This dinner is important."

Henry's mother walked back into his closet. He could hear the motorized tie rack she'd had installed when he began prep school.

"This," she said, handing him a light-yellow tie with tiny little boats on it. He wanted to tell her that he could pick out his own tie. He wanted to tell her that it was okay if he didn't wear one. But he looked into her eyes, so filled with anger and disappointment, and he took the tie from her hands.

"We are leaving in twenty minutes," she said. He nodded back and Ursella left his room.

Henry dressed slowly, the way he did almost everything. He never felt a need to hurry. A lifetime of being waited on had taught him that he needn't rush—the world would wait for Henry Rothschild. Unfortunately for Henry, the world now seemed to be passing him by.

He put on the pants, shirt, and jacket. As he slid his feet into a pair of black loafers, he wondered if she would march him right back into his room to pick out a different pair of shoes for him, too. He made himself laugh, thinking about the fact that she'd also forgotten to select his socks. *Thees is an import-ant dinnare,* he mimicked. *You must be weer-ing the cor-rect socks.*

He checked himself out in the mirror. Pretty good. He and his dad had visited the barber earlier to get haircuts and shaves, and he was pleased with his appearance. He held the yellow tie up to his neck. He thought it made him look weak, like a little boy. He put the tie back, and scanned his tie collection. He stopped when he came to a lavender tie. It matched his outfit—he'd always been taught that lavender works well with charcoal gray—and he had a fleeting thought about the color purple. The color purple, he remembers from his prep school European studies class, is the color of royalty.

This dinner may be important. They may be trying to impress Becca's family. (For what reason, Henry truly didn't know.) But they should be trying to impress him, too. After all, he was, over all else, a Rothschild.

Nineteen

Becca did not like to make people wait for her. She considered lateness to be rude; being late was telling the other party that your time was more valuable than theirs. This was not a message she wanted to send to the Rothschilds. This was why she was already halfway down the stairs when the doorman called to let her know that the Rothschilds were parked outside.

"Get up," Henry's mother told him through closed lips. "Help your girlfriend into the car."

Henry wanted to tell Ursella that there was no need—that his father was already opening the car door—but he didn't want to fight with her. She seemed even more tightly wound than usual today, and Henry was afraid she might break.

Henry stepped out of the car just as Edmond was helping Becca into it. He kissed her awkwardly. What was the protocol in front of one's father? He settled on a chaste kiss on the cheek. He wished that Edmond would loosen his grip on Becca's elbow so that he could help her into the car himself, but Edmond did not, so Henry stood idly by as his father played the perfect gentleman to his girlfriend. Once Becca was situated in the car,

Henry got in. His father sat in the front, next to the driver, and they were off.

Henry looked out his window as the driver made his way toward the West Side Highway. Seeing all of the other cars on the road, he remembered something he used to do on long car rides when he was a little boy. He would take note of the other vehicles close to theirs and keep tabs on them. Which one was in which lane, which got to the traffic lights first. He imagined that they were all in a race, and the one that got to its destination first was the winner.

Young Henry understood that winning was important. The way trophies were displayed. The way certificates were framed. Although nothing compared to the room dedicated to his mother's illustrious ballet career. Photographs and newspaper clippings on the walls, costumes exhibited on mannequins, playbills encased in a glass table.

Before he knew what he was doing, Henry had memorized the color, make, and model of seven different cars, was monitoring which car was in which lane. When their car got in front of all the others, Henry smiled to himself.

"What?" Becca whispered to him.

"Oh nothing," he said, reaching his hands to hers. Becca examined her cuticles. Her thumb had a Band-Aid around it from where she'd bitten a hangnail until it bled.

"How are your studies, dear?" Ursella asked Becca.

As Becca answered Henry's mother, Henry could detect the faint smell of his father's aftershave wafting toward the backseat. It was a smell he associated with his childhood—that faint mix of lemon and verbena that was slapped on after a visit to the barber, and he knew that he probably smelled of it, too, but the odor suddenly suffocated him. He could almost see the scent making its way back—from Edmond's neck in the front seat, over the headrest, and into Henry's unassuming nostrils. It was like a snake, slowly coming at him, winding its way into the backseat and around Henry's neck. He turned his head toward the window, tried to enjoy the view of Yankee Stadium as they made their way north, but the smell. He couldn't get rid of that smell. Coming toward him, enveloping him, attacking him. Henry could barely catch his breath.

He opened his window a crack, and immediately, his mother complained.

"Close that window!" she said. "Are you trying to blow us all away with the wind?"

He turned to face his mother and saw Becca looking at him. Her blond hair was blowing in the breeze, all around her shoulders, like on Botticelli's *Venus*. She wore a tiny smile on her lips. He smiled back.

"I'll put the air on for you," his mother said, and began fiddling with the air vents.

"I just needed some fresh air," Henry said, still looking at Becca, smiling at her. She smiled back at him and tightened her grip on his hand.

"The fresh air feels nice," Becca said.

Ursella agreed to let him keep the window open for the duration of the ride.

Twenty

Valentina got into her Camry and teared up just the tiniest bit. It's okay to feel sorry for yourself, isn't it? As she pulled the car out of the garage, dabbing at her eyes, she realized that the four-inch heels on her boots were making it difficult to drive the car. Her Camry lurched as she hit the gas pedal too hard, and then came to an abrupt stop when she tried to put her foot down on the brake. It was too late to go back into the house to change her shoes—it had taken her over an hour to choose these; God knows how long it would take her to select another pair—so, she did something she'd never done before. She took off her boots and drove barefoot.

Valentina felt a bit silly as she drove down her street. First, there was the fact that she could feel the dirt under her foot as she pressed down on the gas pedal. But what was bothering her, what was really bothering her, was that she was acting like a teenager. It was unbecoming. Especially since she was on her way to Sylvia's house. Sylvia probably never acted like a teenager. Sylvia was classy.

But no one knew she was driving barefoot, acting like some-one who didn't have a mortgage and responsibilities and bills.

And this was a feeling she liked. She glanced at the clock and decided to take the long way to the Golds. The streets would be longer. There would be fewer traffic lights. She turned the radio to a classic rock station. As the Stones' "Gimme Shelter" blared through her speakers, Valentina rolled down the windows, opened the sunroof, and sang along as loudly as she could. And she drove. Fast.

On the sleepy county streets, with the blacktop newly paved, Valentina went faster and faster. Faster than she'd ever driven before. And it felt good.

Yeah, I'm gonna fade away.

She sang with her mouth wide open, oblivious to everything around her. She didn't know the right words, but that didn't stop her. She kept singing.

It's just a kiss away . . .

She was so lost in the music that she didn't even realize that a police car had been trailing her. As the song ended and the DJ went to commercial, she heard the siren blare.

Her first thought was to put her shoes back on. Was it illegal to drive barefoot? She pulled her car over to the side of the road and realized that she'd never been pulled over before. An evening of firsts.

She pulled her feet back toward the seat, trying to hide her bare feet, as the police officer approached her car.

"Do you know why I pulled you over?" he asked, not looking up from the pad he was writing on.

"Danny?" Valentina said. "Is that you?" She wasn't sure, but underneath the police uniform, she could swear it was little Danny Manetti from the neighborhood. She and his mother had been friends back when the boys were in school together. He'd even worked in Dominic's garage for a summer or two in high school.

"Mrs. Russo?" the officer asked. Valentina gave Danny a broad smile. He did not smile back. "I didn't realize it was you."

"How's your mom?" Valentina asked, as if they had just bumped into each other at the library.

"She's good, real good," he said. Valentina noticed the name plate under his badge: Officer Manetti. That was adorable, just adorable. Maybe she shouldn't tell him that. "Do you know you were going sixty-four miles over the speed limit?"

"Well, that can't be," Valentina said. "In this tiny car? I doubt it can even go that fast."

"It does," he said. "It did. I clocked you going ninety-four miles per hour. That's a really big ticket, Mrs. Russo. A lot of points."

"You're not going to give me a ticket, are you?" she said, laughing. "I've known you since you were this high!"

"Once I start writing a ticket," he explained, "I have to issue it."

"How can you give me a ticket?" Valentina pleaded. "You know I just lost Dominic."

"I know, Mrs. Russo, and I was really sorry to hear about that."

"And you're still giving me a ticket?" she demanded. "I'm going to tell your mother about this. Giving a ticket to a woman who just lost her husband."

"With all due respect, Mrs. Russo," Danny said, his eyes firmly planted on his shoes, "he'll be back in two months."

Valentina gasped. "You have no idea—" she began, but Danny cut her off.

Sheepishly, he repeated: "Once I start writing a ticket . . ."

Valentina was too angry to even speak. So many thoughts flooded her mind, she couldn't land on just one.

So instead, she sped away even faster than she'd been driving before. The car screeched as the tires spun wildly on the blacktop. As she turned the radio back up—Led Zeppelin's "Immigrant Song"—she looked out her rearview mirror. She could see Danny's police car, idling at the side of the road. She took the ticket, crumpled it in her hand, and threw it out the sunroof.

Twenty-One

Joe put the roof down on Sarah's convertible; he knew that she wouldn't want to do it herself and risk getting her dress dirty.

The convertible had been a gift for Sarah's college graduation. Joe got it for free when one of his clients couldn't pay his bill. The car was practically a write-off, but somehow Joe got the engine running again. He spent the following year restoring it on nights and weekends. Sarah had no idea it was for her until he painted it red and put a bow on it the day of her graduation. Her friends all thought it was the most romantic thing they'd ever seen.

Sarah didn't think graduating college was a big deal, but that didn't take away from Joe's excitement. College wasn't an option for him. He didn't have the grades, to begin with, and the student loans would have put him in massive debt. No, thank you.

He knew he would take over his father's shop eventually. Why wait? Joe loved cars, he always had. And he loved working alongside his father in his shop. It was a gas station and auto body shop, in business well before there was an Exxon or a Mobil on every corner. Everyone in town was a customer. Dominic had been good to his regulars during the gas crisis in the seventies, and as he used to tell Joe, that's not the sort of thing that people forget.

Dominic ran a true family business. He knew when to let a guy pay in installments because he couldn't afford a bill. He knew when to fix a seventeen-year-old's dented bumper and not tell his old man—and he knew when he should.

Dominic was great with numbers and would run most of the books in his head. Valentina did the books now. Joe had had no idea that his mother was so good with a calculator. But there she was, every Tuesday with her trusty Casio and black composition notebook, as if she'd always been there.

Sarah had rolled her eyes when Joe told her that Valentina was coming every week to take care of the accounts. "Can't you do them yourself?" she'd wondered aloud. Joe wasn't sure if he could or not, but he liked having his mother there. He missed his father in the shop—his loud voice bellowing over the din, his fingers always stained black with grease. It didn't matter how many times he washed them, Dominic's fingers always had a shadow, a faint shade of gray that reminded Joe of what his father did. What he was made of. Joe supposed he was made of the same things. He checked the tips of his fingers often. He was still able to get them clean when he wanted to, but he was just waiting for the day when the pads of his fingers, too, would be marked permanently by the job.

Joe had a plan. A big plan. He may not have gone to college, but he was going to be a big success. A huge success. He would make Sarah and his mother (and even Sarah's mother!) proud. He knew it. He just didn't expect to be putting his plan into motion just yet.

•   •   •

Joe fell in love with his first car when he was six years old. It was a 1969 Corvette Stingray, and his father's friend had won it in a poker game. He'd brought the car to Dominic to see if he could get it running again. Joe loved everything about the car—the color, cherry red, the brightest thing he'd ever seen; the lines, so curvy he could get dizzy just from looking at it; and the most amazing thing of all—it had no roof! Joe would sit inside the car on Sunday mornings—when Dominic would spend the bulk of the day working on it—and pretend to drive. He'd imagine that he was driving along I-95 without a care in the world. Top down, music blasting from the radio, speedometer well past 100 mph.

It wasn't until Joe was eight that Dominic let him help with an actual repair. The first car Joe and Dominic ever revived together was a 1978 Mustang. A couple of teenagers had driven it into a nearby lake, and the owner thought it was beyond repair. Dominic thought it could be a good car to teach Joe on, so he bought it for a song, and began to teach Joe everything he knew.

They put it up on cinder blocks in their driveway. (Oh, how the neighbors must have loved that.) On Sundays when Dominic wasn't in the shop, they'd work on it right out there, in the driveway. Valentina would be inside, cooking Sunday night dinner, the smells of his childhood wafting out to Joe and his father. She'd occasionally bring them a snack or a glass of lemonade. It was the longest Joe had spent with his father. Most of his time was spent with Valentina, hanging around the house or running around town doing errands. His father worked long hours at the shop most days of the week, so it was usually just Joe and his mother. ("The two musketeers, us against the world!" she would often say.)

But those Sundays belonged to Joe and his father. Whenever he felt his father's absence, those were the days he looked back to. Those were the days he'd never forget.

Twenty-Two

"What on earth are you doing up there?"

Sylvia was ten feet in the air, on a ladder, balancing on three-inch heels and sheer force of will.

Their guests would be arriving in half an hour.

"A spiderweb," she said, the anger bubbling. "I found a spiderweb! With insects!"

"Nobody will notice, Syl."

"I noticed," she said. "I noticed."

"Okay, so you noticed. Come down from there."

"My God," Sylvia cried. "What on earth did the painters think they were here for?"

"To paint?"

"Very funny. You know what I mean."

"I don't think they were responsible for pest removal, Syl."

"Well, don't you think they *noticed* it?" Sylvia asked. "Couldn't they have *done something* about it? Or at least *mentioned* it to me?"

"If you think it's bad, I'll call an exterminator next week."

"I didn't say it was bad," Sylvia said, suddenly defensive. "Do you think it's bad?"

She showed him the rag covered with spiderwebs and dead insects.

"I think that it's great. Adds to the charm of the house. Don't old-money people like stuff like that?" Sylvia did not laugh. "You used to laugh at all my jokes," Alan said. "When did you stop laughing at my jokes?"

Sylvia climbed down the ladder. She patted her skirt; it hadn't gotten dirty. She checked her hose; they hadn't run. She inspected her manicure; nary a chip. "I never laughed at your jokes."

Alan held out his hand to his wife, but she hopped off the last rung of the ladder without his assistance.

"If you want to help, put this thing in the laundry room and get the ladder back into the garage," she said, shoving the rag into his hand.

Alan was left to wonder how Sylvia had gotten the ladder out into the entryway in the first place. He took off his tie and his sweater before getting started. The ladder was heavier than he'd anticipated, and he felt a thin layer of sweat forming on his brow as he made his way toward the garage. He placed the ladder against the back wall, next to the worktable he never used, and then looked around the garage for a paper towel to wipe his face. Sylvia would not want to see him sweating.

He couldn't find any paper towels. What he did find, though, was an enormous spiderweb, one that made the spiderweb in the entryway look small and unimportant. It spanned four feet in width, and was just as high. Alan did not want to remove it. It was filled with more insects than the other had been. Larger insects, too.

Insects that looked like they might break away from the web, jump onto his head, and devour him.

He wasn't scared of the bugs. He wasn't. He just didn't want to do it. He looked at his watch and wondered if Joe would be there soon. This was the sort of thing Joe wouldn't think twice about. He did all manner of repairs on the house he shared with Sarah—didn't he once remove a wasp's nest from their mailbox with only a pencil and a dustpan?

Alan recalled the house he had grown up in, how it was always covered in dust, filled with spiderwebs. His mother couldn't clean it properly—her eyes were bad—and she would never allow a stranger into her house to do the job for her.

He was like a little boy stomping his feet: he did not want to clean up this mess. Why should he have to? Anyone who walks out to the garage gets what he deserves for snooping. And anyway, this web was like a work of art, all long lines and glistening in the sun. Almost beautiful, if you could forget what it really was.

A memory: the girls, in elementary school, sent home because they had caught lice. Sharing hats or hairbrushes, probably, but it didn't matter how they had gotten it. It had to be dealt with. Sylvia immediately covered every family member's head with mayonnaise—even her own head, which was lice-free, and Gideon's, also lice-free. She had read in a magazine that when one person in the house has lice (or two, to be more precise), everyone in the house must be treated, just in case.

She had instructed Alan that when he came home, she would cover his head in mayonnaise in the garage, before he walked into the house. He should knock on the garage door when he arrived home, and she would come out to treat him. But that night—wouldn't you know it?—Alan got stuck in the hospital on an emergency shift.

Bedsheets and stuffed animals were washed, couch cushions and pillows were stored in sealed plastic bags, and hair was painstakingly combed out over and over, throughout the course of the following week. Thinking about it made Alan itch.

I am not touching this thing, Alan thought. *I'll call an exterminator tomorrow.* He made his way toward the garage door, and caught sight of the garden hose. An elegant solution. He could get the spiderweb down from the corner, and he didn't have to touch it. He unfurled the hose, pleased with his cleverness, and pulled the trigger.

Before he realized what had happened, Alan was soaked. Covered in swaths of wet spiderweb, covered in a blanket of large insects. He was afraid to open his mouth to yell out in anger, lest a bug enter his mouth.

What Alan hadn't counted on was this: how powerfully the hose would spray. He had imagined a gentle mist, slowly breaking down the web and washing away the dead insects. Instead, a gush of water ricocheted off the back wall and all over Alan's body, bringing the web and its inhabitants down onto him. Alan was covered in it, head to toe.

Sylvia must not know. Alan waited until he heard her footsteps in the kitchen and then darted up the back staircase, stripping his clothes off the second he made it to his bathroom. He got into the shower before even letting the water heat up, and watched the insects pool at the bottom, too large to go down the drain. Alan stood toward the back of the shower, careful not to step on any. He washed his hair twice. He couldn't get it clean enough. And he used Sylvia's loofah all over his body, scrubbing himself until he was raw.

The shower door opened. Sylvia stood, looking at Alan.

"I don't want to talk about it," he said.

"I've laid out fresh clothing for you on the bed," she said. Her eyes moved to the bathtub, where Alan's dirty clothes lay. "The guests will be here in ten minutes."

"I'll be down in eight."

Alan quickly dried himself off. As he dressed, he could still feel the insects all over his body. He imagined them climbing up his legs, covering his arms. Biting the back of his neck.

And he was sure he'd contracted lice.

BOOK TWO

The Last Supper

The second question:
On all other nights we eat all vegetables,
and on this night only bitter herbs.

Twenty-Three

Sarah and Joe quickly found themselves in their usual spots—Joe in the living room with Alan, Sarah in the kitchen with Sylvia. On the short walk to the kitchen, Sarah noticed that the house was different. She didn't know that the gutters had been cleaned, the paint touched up, or new linens acquired. Still, she sensed something in the air.

"Sarah, this is Chef Michael," her mother said, introducing her to the man standing at the kitchen island. He had on a serious-looking chef's coat embroidered with his name.

"You're not cooking?" Sarah asked.

"I thought I'd make things extra special this year," she said.

"Can I sneak a bite of chopped liver before you put it out?" Sarah asked. It was an even trade. If she wouldn't be having her mother's brisket, she could at least console herself with her favorite appetizer.

"Oh, we're not having chopped liver this year, honey."

"Foie gras?" Chef Michael offered, presenting a beautiful tray.

"I don't eat foie gras," Sarah said, and turned to her mother for an explanation.

"It's practically the same thing as chopped liver," Sylvia said. "I just wanted things to be . . . you know . . . slightly elevated."

Sarah clenched her teeth. Sylvia had never invited Joe's parents over for any dinner, much less a holiday dinner, and now she wanted things to be "elevated" for the family of a boy her sister has just met.

"I have the wine right here," Sylvia said.

"Great, thanks," Sarah replied. She glanced at the label: Opus One. Sarah's teeth slowly came together, about to grind, when she thought, *Adult retainer. Adult retainer.*

It wasn't so much that Sylvia had purchased a very expensive bottle of wine on account of the Rothschilds coming to dinner. It was that she'd done her research in doing so. She hadn't bought just any old Rothschild wine, even if it was the most expensive. That would be too easy for Sylvia Gold. No, her mother had obviously taken the time to learn all about the wines of Baron Philippe de Rothschild and how Opus One was his masterpiece collaboration with Robert Mondavi. Becca had been dating Henry Rothschild for only three months and already Sylvia knew all about his family and their various business concerns. Did she even know the first names of Joe's parents?

Sarah took a second to enjoy the Opus One. No point in rushing a two-hundred-dollar bottle of wine, even if she was seething.

"So, what is that thing?" Sylvia asked, pouring herself a glass of wine.

"What thing?" Sarah asked, taking a sip of wine, pretending that she didn't know where her mother was going with this line of questioning.

"That thing around your boyfriend's neck." Sylvia did not like to mince words.

"Oh, it's a lariat," Sarah said, quickly finishing her first glass of wine. She nodded at Chef Michael and he poured her another.

"A lariat?"

"A tie substitute," Sarah said, as nonchalantly as she could muster.

"Excuse me?" her mother asked.

"It's instead of a tie."

Sylvia smiled warmly. "You'll have to tell him to take it off."

"He's wearing it," Sarah said.

Sylvia regarded her daughter for a moment. She was lapping up her wine like a cat would a bowl of warm milk.

Sarah closed her eyes. She would really like to think that her mother does what's best for her, wants what's best for her. But she often thinks that what Sylvia wants is what is best for Sylvia.

"I'd really prefer that he not wear it. This *is* a Seder, after all."

Sarah looked at the fois gras, and the professional chef, and then up at her mother. "This is no longer a Seder. It's a goddamned dinner party."

"An important dinner party."

"You've never invited Joe's parents to an important dinner party."

"Didn't Joe's mother tell you?" Sylvia asked, innocently. "She's coming tonight. I invited her. I was so sorry to hear about her loss."

Sarah hadn't known that Joe's mother was invited. She decided to stick with what she did know: "Joe's dad isn't dead."

"I saw Valentina in the market two weeks ago and she just couldn't stop tearing up about how she'd lost her husband."

"Don't you think that if Joe's father had died, I would have told you about it? Wouldn't you have gone to the funeral?" Sarah asked.

"I just thought you didn't mention it because you know how much I dislike death," Sylvia said. She whispered the word *death*. "So, she's bringing Joe's father? I only have the table set for nine."

"Joe's father isn't coming," Sarah said.

"He left her?" Sylvia asked, ears suddenly perking up at the suggestion of salacious gossip.

"No, Mom," Sarah said. "Joe's father is in jail."

"Oh dear God," her mother said. "That's worse."

"You'd prefer it if he was dead?"

"What are we going to tell the Rothschilds?"

"We're not going to tell them anything," Sarah said.

"What did he do?" Sylvia asked, taking a large swig of wine, fortifying herself for the news.

"It's nothing, really," Sarah explained. "He was out hunting with a cousin, they were both a bit drunk, and he accidentally shot his cousin in the shoulder. His cousin pressed charges for some reason. 'He used malice aforethought!' is what he said, so now Joe's father is serving time. He'll be out soon enough."

"He was hunting?" Sylvia asked. "And drinking? That is so blue collar." She took a big swig of wine for effect.

"Actually, they were hunting, so they were probably wearing plaid."

"You think this is funny?" Sylvia asked.

"No," Sarah said. "I do not think this is funny." But she was very much enjoying the effect the news was having on her mother.

Twenty-Four

"Joe and I were just talking about the shop," Alan said. "Very exciting stuff."

"I'm so happy for him," Sarah replied, and Joe kissed her cheek.

"I couldn't do it without this one," Joe said, putting his arm around her.

What he couldn't do without Sarah was this: open his own auto body shop. And it was true—he couldn't. At least not without the money that Alan had offered. (Alan is a silent partner in the deal.) Joe was turning his father's place into a high-end auto body shop that would do custom jobs on luxury cars. The transition was supposed to happen slowly over the next two years, but with things being what they were, Joe was speeding up the process.

The venture thrills Alan. It embarrasses Sylvia, who sees it as a personal affront.

"It's important to be supportive of your partner," Alan said, glancing toward the kitchen. Sarah's eyes followed his. She noticed the curve in his lip when he caught a glance of Sylvia, bossing Chef Michael around. Sarah wondered why her father was so delighted by this behavior. Sarah, herself, didn't appreciate it. But as she caught a glimpse of Chef Michael, bowing to Sylvia's every whim, she realized that he didn't seem to mind it, either. Found it charming, even. Perhaps Sarah was the only one who buckled under the strain of the "Gold Standard," as Sylvia called it.

"Hell-oooo!" Valentina's voice broke through Sarah's train of thought. Sarah hadn't realized that her father and Joe were having an in-depth conversation about the subprime mortgage crisis and what that would do to small businesses. And she hadn't heard the door open.

Valentina Russo was nothing if not distracting. She always looked like she was in the center of a tornado—all wild, curly black hair blowing in the breeze, and a frenetic aura that would make your blood pressure speed up just from standing next to her.

"Tina, you made it," Alan said, rushing to take her wrap and the bottle of wine she'd brought.

"It's kosher," she said. "I went to three different places to find the right one for Passover."

"That is so kind of you," he said, as they kissed on the cheek.

"Joey!" she called out, grabbing Joe for an enormous bear hug. He was her only child and it showed.

"Hey, Ma." Joe let his mother hug him for a long time. Longer, in Sarah's opinion, than was necessary.

Then, she turned to Sarah. "My daughter!" she called out and enveloped her in a hug.

"They're not married yet," Sylvia trilled from the kitchen.

"Oh, right," Valentina said, winking at Sarah. "I just wish she were my daughter. You are so lucky, Sylvia."

"Thank you, Tina," Sylvia said. She gave Valentina a tiny

peck on the cheek, as if she were afraid of getting too close. "You're very sweet."

"Sylv, Tina brought kosher wine," Alan said, holding up the bottle. "Wasn't that thoughtful?"

"It was," Sylvia said, her face straining to smile. "But, unfortunately, we're serving the wine that the Rothschilds produce."

She said it as though this were a restaurant and the decision was simply out of her hands.

"Oh, that's okay," Valentina said, seemingly unoffended by Sylvia's lack of social grace. "We can drink it next year!"

Twenty-Five

"What is that?" Sylvia asked, even though she knew. The smell was singular, for one. And there was simply no mistaking what was on the plate.

"Frog legs," Chef Michael said, smiling, as he poured a gentle butter sauce onto his creation.

Sylvia stared at the serving platter. The legs were arranged artfully, splayed out as if ready to jump. They looked suspended in motion, as if they'd hopped into the deep fryer that way. Sylvia grasped the kitchen island; she felt unsure on her feet.

"Frogs were one of the plagues inflicted on Pharaoh," Chef Michael said. He did not notice the reaction Sylvia was having to his starter course. Frog legs were a delicacy, surely a woman like Sylvia knew that?

"I know why you did it," Sylvia said. "I just don't know *why* you did it."

"I thought it would be fun to be playful with the menu."

"I did not tell you to be playful with the menu," Sylvia said. She sat down in a chair, certain she would faint.

"When we discussed the menu," Chef Michael said, "I mentioned that I'd prepare a few little surprises for you. When you're the hostess, it's hard to be surprised. But you should get to be a guest at your own party, too."

"I'm the hostess precisely because I don't want any surprises," Sylvia said.

Chef Michael did not know how to respond. Sylvia continued: "I thought the little surprises would be things like gribenes, those crispy chicken and fried onion bits my mother used to sneak into the middles of matzoh balls."

"I have matzoh balls."

"With gribenes?"

"No," Chef Michael said. "What are they again?"

"Never mind," Sylvia said. "Get rid of the frogs."

What Sylvia wanted to do was to march out of the kitchen for effect. To walk right out on Chef Michael, mid-conversation. Frog legs! What sort of sick joke was that?

But she couldn't. She wouldn't.

What's more, Valentina had just walked in and she seemed to think that this year's invite to the Seder meant that she now had a standing invitation to attend the Gold family Seder every year, from here on out. What was that expression about no good deed going unpunished? Sylvia should never have been so kind.

Valentina took a look around the house. *So, this is what they've been hiding from me all these years,* she thought. *It's not so special.* Everything was beige. The walls were beige, the couches were beige. Even the rug was a slightly darker shade of beige. She watched enough HGTV to know that you needed to have a pop of color in every room. Surely Sylvia knew that as well? Valentina made a mental note to buy Sylvia an orange throw blanket for the living room this year for Christmas.

"Your home is beautiful," Valentina said to Alan. It was the appropriate thing to say in the situation. Classy people didn't say anything about their hosts dying a slow death amongst the beige.

"Can I show you around?" Alan asked. "I just realized that you've never been here before."

"No, I haven't," she said, still looking around the entryway. From the vestibule she could see the living room, the dining room, and a tiny bit of the kitchen. How much beige could one person look at before losing her mind?

Valentina couldn't think of a nice way to tell Alan that she'd seen quite enough, thank you, so she let him guide her around. She was careful not to touch anything. Sylvia, it seemed to her, was the type who would have a "you break it, you bought it" policy.

Each room had a story, some old piece of furniture that Sylvia had "discovered" while they were antiquing in some far-off land. Valentina knew that this was the part where she was supposed to be impressed, but she really couldn't understand what was so great about taking old stuff that had once belonged to someone else. They did that in her family all the time and they never made a big stink about it.

Every room was pristine—it looked like no one really lived there. Valentina much preferred a house that looked lived in. That had soul. The only soul that Sylvia's house had was by way of an antique sewing machine she had on display in her bedroom's sitting room. Sylvia didn't even sew.

Alan was proud of his home. It was as if he thought Sylvia had invented the concept of putting a rug on a hardwood floor.

"I'd love to have you over to my house one of these days," Valentina said. She knew Sylvia would never accept her invitation, and she just couldn't resist asking.

"That would be lovely," he said. "I'll let you and Sylvia work out a date."

As they made their way downstairs, Valentina could smell dinner cooking. That was one thing that Sarah always bragged about—her mother's cooking. Valentina couldn't wait to try her brisket. She was certain it wasn't better than her own pot roast, even though whenever she asked Joe about it, he would say that there was no way to compare, they were just too different.

"I have a surprise for everyone," Valentina announced as they approached Sarah and Joe in the living room.

"What kind of surprise?" Alan asked.

"Well, then, it wouldn't be a surprise if I told you now, would it?" Valentina replied, putting her index finger out to tap him on the nose, as if he were a toddler. But he didn't mind. Valentina spoke breathlessly, as if she was Marilyn Monroe singing "Happy birthday, Mr. President." It had an effect on men of a certain age. Valentina knew this.

"I suppose it wouldn't," he said. "Wine?"

"Yes," Valentina, Joe, and Sarah all said in unison.

"Did I hear something about a surprise?" Sylvia asked, rushing out from the kitchen, glass of wine in hand.

"Well, I really wanted to wait until everyone was here," Valentina said, barely suppressing her joy. If she were a balloon, she would have burst.

"You don't have to wait," Sylvia said. Her face was a stone. Her eyes were set, angry even, and her lips formed a straight line.

The tension she held in her mouth was so full, so deep, that Sarah thought it could only be released if Valentina announced that the surprise was that she was leaving the house this very minute.

"I have an idea," Joe said. "Why don't you tell me privately and then I'll decide if we should tell the group now. Or even at all."

"Why don't you tell us all now," Sylvia said, only it didn't come out as a question, more like a command.

"Well, I've been talking to the warden."

Sylvia gasped.

"And he's agreed to let us do a video chat with Dominic before the Seder tonight!"

"Oh my God," Sylvia said. Her face lost its color.

Joe looked at Sarah with a face that said, *I promise I had no idea about any of this.*

"I think it's lovely," Alan said. "If Dominic can't be with us for the Seder, the very least we can do is try to bring the Seder to him."

"I agree," Sarah said as she gave Joe's hand a little squeeze.

"Then, it's settled," Alan said.

"Settled," Sylvia replied. "Right."

"Great," Alan said.

"Although," Sylvia said, slowly, tentatively, like a lion stalking its prey, "we wouldn't want to make the Rothschilds uncomfortable in any way."

"No, we wouldn't," Valentina agreed.

"How would this make the Rothschilds uncomfortable?" Sarah asked.

"You know," she said. "All of the lawsuits." She whispered the word *lawsuits* as if it were something communicable, like smallpox.

"What lawsuits?" Sarah asked.

"Yes, Sylv," Alan chimed in. "What lawsuits?"

"I'm not even sure we should be talking about this," she said. "I mean, it's simply rude to talk about other party guests before they've arrived."

"Make an exception," Alan said, the smile leaving his eyes.

"Some people are saying that the Rothschilds are connected to that whole Bernie Madoff mess," she said. "I wouldn't want them thinking about jail when they could be going to jail themselves!"

"I completely understand," Valentina said, and made a big show of hiding her iPad under her sweater.

"Thank you." Sylvia grabbed Valentina's hand. "Thank you for your discretion."

Sylvia may have thought this conversation was over, but it was not.

"There is no pending litigation against the Rothschilds," Alan said. "Who told you such utter nonsense?"

"Google," Sylvia said, shrugging her shoulders. Valentina watched, wondering who would win this battle of wills. She had a sense that Sylvia ruled this house, but this argument would determine who was really in charge.

"May I please speak with you privately?" Alan didn't give his wife a chance to respond. He cupped his hand under her elbow and steered her toward the kitchen.

But they didn't get very far. Halfway across the family room, the doorbell rang.

Twenty-Six

And then it happened. The air suddenly changed. Everyone held their breath for a moment. The night was about to start.

The Rothschilds had arrived.

"They're here!" Sylvia screamed, breaking free from Alan's grip. "They're here! Everyone . . ."

"Should we hide?" Joe whispered to Sarah. "Are we supposed to yell 'surprise'?"

Sarah quietly giggled as Alan tried to calm Sylvia down. "How wonderful!" he said, his hand still firmly placed on her elbow. "Everyone, just relax as we go and answer the door."

Sylvia and Alan walked toward the door, Sylvia wiping imaginary dust off every surface she passed.

"Is it the queen of England?" Valentina whispered to Joe, who immediately looked to Sarah. Sarah smiled at him—permission to laugh. She felt for him at times like these.

Becca ran to Sarah with a bear hug that nearly knocked her older sister down.

"Sarah! I haven't seen you in so long," she said.

"It's so good to see you, Rebecca."

And then, the introductions. First Edmond, the Boyfriend's father. He made it a point to introduce himself to everyone in the family room and to shake each hand, look each person in the eyes.

"Nice to meet you, Sylvia."

"Nice to meet you, Valentina."

"Nice to meet you, Sarah."

Next, Ursella, the Boyfriend's mother. "Hello," she said to everyone in her heavily accented English. Alan tried to place the accent, but Sylvia already knew, courtesy of her Google search: Russia.

And then, finally, the Boyfriend. Sarah didn't know what to make of him. He didn't look like Rebecca's other boyfriends, which is to say, tall, dark, and handsome. This one looked different. He was blond haired and blue eyed, like a Ralph Lauren model. And his smile. His smile was so bright, it couldn't possibly be real.

"What?" Becca whispered to Sarah. She could tell something was wrong.

"Nothing," Sarah whispered back. "He seems nice. They all seem nice."

Becca pulled Sarah into their father's study.

"But you don't like him," she accused.

"I don't even know him!" Sarah said. "I've barely said five words to him. He's very handsome."

"You think he's too handsome," she said.

"No," Sarah said. "Why don't we go back inside so I can get to know him a bit better?"

"Have you spoken with Gid?"

"We video chatted the other day," Sarah said. "The holidays make me miss him."

"Me, too," Becca said. "Even though we hate him."

"You don't have to like someone to love them."

Twenty-Seven

When it came to house tours, Ursella was an expert. (*Town &
Country* had photographed her home three times. *Architectural
Digest*—once.) But of this Alan had no idea. Instead of a "nice
view of the backyard," he should have described the "sweeping view of the nearby lake." Instead of "Sylvia picked out all of
the bedding," he should have known that his duvet was bespoke
Egyptian cotton, with a six-hundred-thread count. Instead of "a
decent-sized bathtub," he should have talked about the oversized
Jacuzzi, large enough for two.

But Ursella didn't care about any of those things. What she
cared about, what she wanted to see, was Becca's room. Ursella
liked Becca. She liked her a lot. She certainly liked her more
than the girls Henry usually brought home. Girls who would be
better left outside. Better suited to cleaning their toilets. Becca
was different. For one, she had already graduated college—usually
Henry liked to date girls who were younger than he was. She was
poised. Most of Henry's ex-girlfriends chewed gum and flipped
their hair with alarming frequency. But what really excited Ursella was the fact that Becca went to medical school. She was

smart. She was going places. A girl like Becca could make Henry a better man.

Or at least Ursella hoped she could. But she needed to see Becca's bedroom to figure out if she was right about her. Perhaps, like her Henry, Becca merely looked the part. Maybe once you peeled back the first layer, you'd find that she was no different from the girls Henry usually dated, just in a better outfit.

Ursella let out a tiny sigh. She hadn't meant to do it, but she had been holding her breath since leaving Manhattan. She'd only just realized it. Becca's room was just what Ursella had hoped for. The room exuded a pale-pink innocence. High school mementos littered the walls. A bouquet of dried roses was displayed on the bedside table. Stuffed animals were huddled on the ivory bedspread. Ursella smiled to herself. Yes, Becca would do just fine. Alan pretended to be humble when he showed off Becca's embarrassment of trophies and achievements. First place in a gymnastics tournament. Second place in a storytelling competition. Five first-place trophies stacked neatly in a row from tennis matches. But Ursella knew he enjoyed bragging. Why shouldn't he? If Ursella had such a child, she would yell it from the rooftops.

Ursella looked up from the trophy case and her eyes met Edmond's. He, too, had noticed that Becca's room was a shrine to perfection. He nodded at his wife. Ursella smiled in return, certain that they were thinking the same thing.

They were not.

For Ursella, it was enough that Becca be a good influence on Henry. The dog-eared copies of *The Catcher in the Rye* and *To*

Kill a Mockingbird, the high school letters from various sports played and mastered, the framed letters of commendation from the dean. This was the sort of girl Henry needed. Please let her stay around long enough to get Henry interested in re-enrolling in school. Or getting a job. Or doing anything besides padding around her town house all day.

Edmond needed more. But Ursella didn't know that just yet. No one knew that just yet. (But more on that later.)

For Ursella, Becca would do just fine.

Twenty-Eight

"May I have your attention?" Sylvia clinked her wineglass with a tiny spoon. "Chef Michael will be serving the wine."

Becca shot Sarah a look.

Sarah shot one back.

Chef Michael made a big show of pouring the wine properly, explaining how he'd poured the wine properly, and then, after he had poured the wine properly, telling the guests that they were drinking Opus One.

"Is that one of ours?" the Boyfriend's mother asked.

"Yes, sweetheart," the Boyfriend's dad responded. "How lovely, Sylvia."

"How cute," the Boyfriend's mother agreed, and Sylvia winced. With Ursella's accent it sounded like: *how coot*. As in: *what a coot!* Sylvia did not like to be described as cute. Or coot. She liked sweeping adjectives. Adjectives that were grand in stature. Adjectives that conveyed exactly how important Sylvia Gold was. Cute was not such an adjective.

"Thank you," she responded with a tight smile.

Chef Michael then set out the foie gras and toast points, along with Sylvia's newly purchased linen napkins.

Sylvia nodded her approval while Chef Michael continued his presentation with passed service—potato pancakes, placed beautifully on one of Sylvia's sterling silver trays. Only these weren't your regular potato pancakes, fried lovingly until crisp and served with a generous dollop of applesauce. No, these were fancy-chef potato pancakes. An "interpretation" of a potato pancake. Chef Michael was explaining this to a very doubtful Sarah (it involved something called a "deconstruction"), who stuffed one into her mouth for the sole purpose of shutting him up.

Sarah turned away to chew, hoping this would signal Chef Michael to stop talking. (It did not.) She was disappointed in the pancake. It tasted nothing like the potato pancakes she had grown up on. The ones she would make on the stove top with her mother, wearing an apron that was too big, Sylvia pulling her back any time she felt the oil splatters getting too high. The potatoes in Chef Michael's dish were separated from the matzo meal, and he used real apples instead of applesauce for that taste of sweetness. Sarah spit it out into her embroidered linen napkin.

Sylvia was ever-so-gently steering Valentina away from Ursella. She did that whenever the women got within five feet of each other. But Valentina didn't notice. After all, she didn't care about Becca's boyfriend or his parents, Rothschild or not. All she ever cared about was Joe.

Valentina doted on Joe, running her fingers through his hair, wiping imaginary dirt from his face, brushing her hands across his broad shoulders. Sarah often joked that if he were to let her, she might even try to feed him.

After "cocktail hour," Sylvia ushered her guests to the dining room. The table was set with her good china, yet more linen napkins, and something their family had never used before: place cards.

"Ooh, I'm next to you, Alan," Valentina cooed.

"I am as well," Ursella said, sitting in the chair to Alan's right, at the head of the table.

"Lucky me," Alan said. "I've got the best seat in the house."

"So do I," Sylvia said, showing the Boyfriend's father to his seat, the one to the right of her place at the head of the table. The Boyfriend was seated to her left.

The table was rounded out like this: Rebecca next to the Boyfriend; Joe and Sarah across the table from each other; Joe next to his mother; and Sarah in between her sister and the Boyfriend's mom. Sarah hated that she and Joe were not sitting next to each other. She looked down as she carefully, slowly took out her cell phone to text Joe.

"Absolutely not," Sylvia said, catching Sarah as she tapped away under her linen napkin. "Phones away," she scolded. Even though this comment was meant only for Sarah, the Rothschilds all dutifully took their phones out and turned them off.

Valentina did not. In fact, almost as if to show just what she thought of this no-phones-at-the-Seder-table rule, her phone began to chirp.

"I'll just answer this real quick," she stage-whispered to Sylvia. She tried to keep her voice down, but it was no use. Everyone at the table was looking at her, waiting to find out who was on the other end of the line. "I should have let you know. We've decided not to take the call."

Then, she stage-whispered to Sylvia: "It's the warden. I'm taking care of it now."

"The warden?" Ursella asked. "What are you taking care of?"

"We were going to do a video chat with Joe's dad," she said. "On account of his good behavior. Joe's dad's, I mean, not Joe's! Joe's not even in prison!"

"Prison?" Becca repeated, and looked to Sarah for an explanation.

"Well, that sounds love-eh-lee," Mrs. Rothschild said, not skipping a beat. "Why are you canceling that?"

"Oh, Sylvia thought it wouldn't be a good idea. We don't want to upset anyone. You know, especially given your family's history."

"*Excuse me?*"

Mr. Rothschild, who hadn't really been paying attention to this whole exchange, turned to hear the answer to his wife's question. He looked a bit pale.

"This is just a big misunderstanding!" Sylvia trilled from the edge of the table. "Of course we're having the video chat! Tina, you must have misunderstood me."

"I did?" Joe's mom asked, and looked to Joe. Joe looked at Sarah. Sarah, in turn, looked back at both of them and tried to formulate a thought. But the wine wouldn't let her.

"Of course you did!" Sylvia said. Everything Sylvia was saying was so emphatic that Sarah furrowed her brow, wondering if her mother might explode from the sheer force of her words. "Go get your iPad! I insist!"

Valentina looked to Alan. "She insists," he said.

Valentina got up slowly and walked toward the door. Moments later, she returned to the table with her iPad.

"Chef Michael!" Sylvia called out. "I think we're all going to need another glass of wine."

Twenty-Nine

"Can you hear me now? Can you hear me now?"

It was not a promising start. Valentina could barely get her iPad to connect. Every time she thought she was connected, that spinning beach ball returned to the center of her screen to say otherwise.

"Alan has an enormous computer in his home office," Sylvia said, under the guise of being helpful. "Maybe you'd get a better connection there?"

Alan shot a look to Sylvia that was roughly the equivalent of giving her the middle finger. She smiled back: *You can't blame a girl for trying.* Alan's face turned to a soft, mushy smile.

"Let me take a look," he said, and fidgeted with the iPad until the video chat came in loud and clear.

"Where's my daughter-in-law?" Dominic asked. "I want to see my daughter-in-law."

"They're not married!" Sylvia trilled.

"Hi, Dom," Sarah said.

"Beautiful!" he said. "You look so beautiful. *Mazel tov!*"

Mazel tov wasn't exactly the correct expression, but Sarah found it so endearing that he tried to be appropriate to the occasion that she didn't have the heart to correct him.

"A *zissen Pesach*," Alan said. "Happy Passover."

"Alan!" Dominic said, as Sarah passed the iPad to Alan. "A decent pay sock to you, too!"

"You okay in there?" Alan asked.

"Oh yes, fine," he said, as if he were staying in a three-star hotel, and not his usual four-star. "Where's my bride?"

"I'm right here, honey!" Valentina said, reaching across Alan to take the iPad from him. "I miss you so much, Nicky."

"Beautiful!" he said. "You look so beautiful. Where's my boy?"

"Hey, Pop." Joe looked slightly embarrassed by this whole exchange, but the Rothschilds sat smiling, enjoying this bit of computer-assisted family time.

"You taking care of the shop?"

"Yeah, Pop."

"Good," he said. "I want you to be a big success like your little lady."

Sarah couldn't help but smile when Dominic said things like that. He meant it with good, old-fashioned love. Surely Anna Wintour allowed a "little lady" to slip by here and there?

Moments later, Joe was waving the iPad around, submitting to his father's request to "show me all of the beautiful people there at the table."

"Gorgeous!" Dominic said. "Just gorgeous! Every single one of you is gorgeous!"

•   •   •

Dominic never met a person who didn't like him. He noticed it at a young age—that he was able to make men like him and women fall in love with him with little to no effort. He didn't know what it was, but guessed that it was something in his face. It looked honest, his father had told him, the kind of face you could trust.

But this was a new experience, being in prison. He was finding that he couldn't win people over with just a charming smile. If he resorted to his regular trick, the one he'd taught Joe—show them your teeth—his teeth were very likely to get kicked out. And Dominic did not want his teeth to get kicked out.

Everyone he encountered there was inclined to hate him. He thought he'd be able to win over the prison guards with his charm, but that wasn't how things worked inside. Not even at a minimum-security prison. Everything on the inside worked on favors.

What can you do for me?

What can you get for me?

How can you help me?

But Dominic didn't have anything to give. In the real world, he owned a business. He did people favors. He helped people out. But inside, he was finding it hard.

He could have asked Valentina to bring him things to trade, but he wanted her to think he was all right. He didn't want her to know the way things really were.

The female guards offered sex for money, the warden was a sadist who enjoyed watching inmates fight, and things were being sent in and out of the kitchen at an alarming rate. Dominic had been assigned to laundry duty, the least scandalous place there was. He thanked his lucky stars for small miracles.

Valentina came to visit every week, just like she'd promised, and Dominic was sure to put on a happy face for her. When she convinced the warden to let her do a video chat—at a Gold family holiday, no less!—he didn't have the heart to say no. He could never say no to Valentina.

He only hoped that Joe would forgive him.

"So nice to meet you, Dominic," the Boyfriend's father said to the iPad. "We look forward to meeting you in person soon."

"Classy!" Dominic said. "Youse all are some classy folks!"

At this, Joe's face turned a slight shade of red. Sarah moved her foot to his leg, a show of support, but she hit the leg of the table instead.

LOVE YOU, she texted under the table. Joe reached for his pants, saw the message, and smiled.

Dominic continued going on about how gorgeous everyone at the table was; no one seemed to mind. Even Sylvia realized that it must be refreshing to see something normal after being in jail for a few weeks. There probably wasn't anything beautiful to see in that prison, and it probably felt good for Dominic to remember that there was a whole life waiting for him when he got out. After all, even a minimum-security prison was still a prison.

The warden came back to announce that the chat was over. Valentina put the iPad away. Sylvia let out a deep breath. It was as if she'd been holding her breath this entire time. Which she had been.

"Now," she said, "shall we begin?"

Thirty

Depending on who leads a Passover Seder, it can go one of two ways. It can be a long and somewhat depressing service. (Slavery. Ten plagues brought upon the land. The slaying of all firstborn children.) Or, it can, in the right hands, be a joyous family celebration. (Four cups of wine. A children's song about Moses floating in a basket. A sandwich made out of apples, walnuts, red wine, and cinnamon.)

Every Jewish family conducts its Seder in its own way. Some strive to make the ceremony as precise as possible. They do not skip pages; they sing every song. They lean when the Haggadah says to lean, wash hands when it says to wash hands, and they do not dare drink wine unless the text specifically says to do so.

The Gold family, too, had its own distinct kind of Seder. Year after year, they would sing a song about the plagues—a holdover from Gideon's childhood days when he'd learned a nursery school song about jumping frogs—and drink wine whenever they felt like it. They would sneak bites of matzoh before the Haggadah called for it, because even though matzoh tastes like cardboard, anything is better than giving your full attention to the service at hand.

Sylvia knew this—she'd hop up from the table like a jumping frog under the pretense of checking on the food at regular intervals. Sarah always tagged along—the self-appointed marshmallow police, making sure the top of the sweet potato casserole was caramelized just the right amount. With the addition of Chef Michael to the holiday, Sylvia would have no choice but to stay at the table for the entire service. Sarah wondered if that meant that she, too, would have to stay put like a dinner party guest, as opposed to a member of the family.

At this evening's Seder, there was to be no silly singing, no matzoh sneaking, no furtive drinking. Alan sat a little higher in his seat; Sylvia left her wineglass untouched. Sarah could tell that the Rothschilds, too, were taking this Seder more seriously than need be. Ursella took out one set of reading glasses for herself and passed another to her husband. Edmond flipped through the pages of the Haggadah, readying himself. Valentina, upon seeing this, paged through her own Haggadah. Joe silently took the book from his mother's hands and showed her how to open it from left to right, as opposed to the other way around, which had caused her book to begin at the end.

Everyone was solemn.

Sarah was not. She put her napkin in her lap, ready to eat even though the service did not allow for it until page twenty-seven. She would not sit up straight in her seat. She would not page through her Haggadah. She spooned a bite of charoset onto her plate and scooped it up with a piece of matzoh, which she washed down with a generous sip of wine. Copious amounts of wine were in order if Sarah was expected to get through this Seder.

"Sarah, what are you doing?" Sylvia asked. Alan continued with the service, unruffled, giving it his full attention. He was Sylvia's devoted rabbi, the Moses to her God, fully committed to the task at hand.

"Are we not up to this part?" Sarah stage-whispered back to her mother. Sylvia shook her head and Sarah couldn't help but giggle. How many glasses of wine had she had? She couldn't recall.

Joe furrowed his brow. Was he kidding? *He* wanted her to take this Seder more seriously? He wasn't even Jewish. *You aren't even Jewish!* she telegraphed with her eyes. But apparently Joe wanted to please Sylvia, just like everyone else.

Sarah put her head back down into her Haggadah.

The table was set with the traditional trappings of a Passover Seder—the matzoh, the Seder plate, and the glass that would later be filled with wine for Elijah.

When Sarah was a little girl, she had no idea that the wineglass was a symbol. She truly believed that the prophet was coming to visit, that he would redeem the Golds, as God had promised Moses. It wasn't until high school that she realized that it was her father who quickly downed the wine when the family was up at the buffet dinner.

Sarah was so lost in thought that she didn't notice that Alan had handed over the reins to Joe, who was now reading from the Haggadah. He was reading in English, not Hebrew, but still, that he was reading at all broke Sarah's train of thought. And he was taking the whole thing so very seriously. There he was, holding his Haggadah with both hands, like a little child, reading the passage:

> This is the bread of affliction that our fathers ate in the land of Egypt. Whoever is hungry, let him come and eat; whoever is in need, let him come and conduct the Seder of Passover. This year we are here; next year in the land of Israel. This year we are slaves; next year we will be free people.

Joe had been coming to family Seders since he was young, but Sarah wasn't at all aware that he'd been paying such close attention. Alan held up the matzoh and handed it to Joe, who then broke the middle piece.

"Bravo!" Valentina said. She clapped as if Joe were a five-year-old just learning to read.

Alan then asked the Boyfriend's father to continue reading the next passage.

Under the table, Sarah texted Joe: WHAT THE HELL WAS THAT?

He texted back: I THOUGHT YOU'D BE HAPPY?

They looked up at each other and Joe smiled. He didn't show a mouthful of teeth, so Sarah knew he was being sincere.

Thirty-One

"The Four Questions," the Boyfriend's father announced.

And with that, a memory: a Passover table filled with distant cousins, people Sarah barely knew. Old women wearing wigs who pinched her cheeks, who left her with bright-pink lipstick stains all over her face. Men wearing brown pants and wide ties who asked if she knew who they were (she did not). Cousins who were just a few years older than she was who wore miniskirts and tight sweaters, and had their hair teased high. They looked like adults. Sarah still very much felt like a child. Her placement at the "kiddie table" with Becca saw to that. Gideon got to sit with the adults.

Sarah had been attending Hebrew school for two years, preparing for her Bat Mitzvah. But she couldn't retain anything. She couldn't understand how to read Hebrew (even with constant tutoring from Gideon) and she kept forgetting to read right to left. It didn't matter anyway, Sarah couldn't remember any of the Hebrew characters or how to incorporate the vowels, which hovered around the letters like Morse code. She hated attending classes. She would humiliate herself by opening the textbook from the left side, not the right, seemingly the only person in the class who made this error week after week. The teacher was mean and called on her all the time—just for the pleasure of humiliating her.

Before the Seder, Sarah had told her mother that she couldn't recite the Four Questions. She begged her to let Gideon do it instead, as he always had.

No.

"Come by me, *bubbala*," her grandfather said. "I want to hear you sing."

Sarah froze. She tried to read the Hebrew text, but the characters all danced around each other, merging into one. In a panic, she attempted to read the English phonetic transliteration of the Hebrew words, but still couldn't seem to figure out how to pronounce each word.

With everyone's eyes on her, Sarah looked up to her mother. Sylvia looked back at her and smiled. She wanted so badly for Sarah to be able to do it. Perhaps if she wanted it badly enough, it would come to be?

Sarah's eyes teared up. She looked up at her mother to explain, but then Becca began to sing. Slowly, at first, but then with confidence. She knew the entire song, all Four Questions, and with her perfect voice she sang it perfectly. As if there were any other way.

Sarah was eleven.

Becca was eight.

How was her sister able to read the questions? Had she been paying attention all those evenings when Gideon tutored Sarah? Or had she simply memorized them, after hearing them read aloud year after year? Sarah was never sure.

The following week, Sarah stopped going to Hebrew school. Her mother would still drop her off for classes, but Sarah would hide out for their duration at the pizza place down the street from their temple. And Becca took over the duties of the Four Questions.

"You're up, kiddo," Alan said to Becca.

"Actually," the Boyfriend's mother's said, "Henry is younger than Rebecca."

"He is?" Sylvia asked.

"Oh, I thought I mentioned that," Becca said, almost under her breath.

"It doesn't really matter," Alan said. "Let's continue with the service."

But no one wanted to continue with the service. All anyone wanted to do was find out how old, exactly, Henry was.

Sarah's cell phone buzzed in her lap. Joe's text: JAIL-BAIT?!

Sarah pressed her lips together so as not to laugh. She looked to Henry, who was poised to start the Four Questions.

"So, how old *are* you?" Valentina blurted out.

Henry had already decided that he did not like this woman. Who was she, anyway, and what was she doing here? As far as he could tell, Becca's sister was dating her son. Sylvia had made it abundantly clear that she didn't like Joe, so why was his mother invited?

And that nonsense with the video chat with the jail. Jail! Her husband was in jail! Could it get any more blue?

"I'm twenty," Henry said to Valentina. They locked eyes and Henry dared her to challenge him again.

"A college man," Alan said. "Rebecca just graduated, so there's barely a difference, is there?"

"Yeah, twenty's not that much younger than twenty-two," Sarah piped in, trying to salvage the situation. She could see Becca's cheeks burning and wanted to help her sister out. "What school are you attending?"

"I'm not going to college," he said.

Henry wondered why it had been so important for him to get up to speed on everyone at the table—Sarah's in fashion, Alan's in medicine, Sylvia does charity work—but no one had taken the time to find out anything about his life.

Sarah could feel the heat coming off Sylvia's body all the way down the table.

"Oh, that's cool," Sarah said on reflex. Not because she thought it was, but because she didn't know exactly what to say.

"My Joey didn't go to college," Valentina said, putting her hands all over Joe. "And look at how good he turned out! As long as you work hard, you can own your own business one day, like my Joey."

"I'm not working right now," Henry said. He said it very matter-of-factly, without embarrassment, without shame. As if this were a perfectly acceptable thing to say, without qualification. As if twenty-year-olds everywhere neither worked nor attended school. As if he didn't need to explain what it was he did all day.

And because he was a Rothschild, he didn't.

Thirty-Two

Sylvia liked to get what she wanted. Preschool, for example. Even though she was a little relieved to be out of Manhattan where it wasn't unheard of to hire a coach for preschool admission, she still enrolled her children in the most prestigious nursery school she could find. Summercrest Country Day School was the most expensive in the area, for one, and the curriculum (Alan had balked at the word) was unparalleled. The children were taught piano when they turned three. They studied the Impressionists in art class. They planted vegetables and herbs in the teaching garden. They learned how to play chess. Gideon had been a huge success at Summercrest. His teachers fawned all over him.

He's already learned his letters and numbers.

He is so interested in reading!

He is the best-behaved child in our class.

Things were different with Sarah. She wouldn't leave her mother's side. She had to be dragged into the classroom, kicking and screaming, until a teacher could pry her off her mother's body. Once they got her into class, Sarah cried hysterically for the first half hour, until she could be distracted by arts-and-crafts time.

After her first year of nursery school, Sylvia expected that Sarah would be placed in the same pre-K class as her brother. All of the parents at school knew that Miss Mindy was the best teacher; they fought to have their children placed in her class. Not Sylvia. She didn't have to. Her daughter was a legacy. Which was why Sylvia wasn't anxious when she received the class assignments in the mail. Which was why she was shocked to learn that Sarah had been placed in Miss Darlene's class.

"Miss Darlene is where the dumb kids go," she told the director of the school the following morning.

"There are no dumb kids at this school," the director said, closing the door behind Sylvia so that the other mothers wouldn't hear their conversation.

"Everyone knows that the gifted children go to Miss Mindy's class."

"That's not really true," the director said carefully. "I thought that Sarah would be a better fit with Miss Darlene. She loves arts-and-crafts time, and Miss Darlene does a lot of her lessons through art."

"Why isn't she a good fit for Miss Mindy?" Sylvia demanded. "Gideon was a good fit for Miss Mindy."

"Every child is different," the director explained.

"I have three children," Sylvia said. "You don't have to tell me that children are different. I know that."

The director didn't respond. After all, what could she say? She very well couldn't convince Sylvia that Miss Darlene's class wasn't for the "dumb" kids any more than she could explain why Gideon and Sarah were different. Sylvia knew they were different—she had to know, didn't she?—but she remained firm, fingering the three-carat diamond studs in her ears, her jaw set. Sylvia's mouth was smiling, but her eyes were not.

After ten minutes of silence, when the director couldn't take any more of Sylvia's glare, she agreed to move Sarah into Miss Mindy's class.

"The importance of charity work cannot be overstated," Sylvia said from her end of the table. Sylvia was trying to bail Henry out, but Sarah knew that it was already too late for that. Sylvia never stopped fighting, though. She never did. That was one thing that Sarah knew about her mother. Sarah would have been surprised if Sylvia *hadn't* tried to intervene on Henry's behalf.

Sylvia had committed herself to the idea of Henry. He was a Rothschild, after all, and Sarah knew that this was, for some reason, important to her mother. Sylvia had decided that Henry was right for Becca, and she wasn't going to let anything, least of all a little setback like the fact that he appeared to be a lazy dilettante, change her mind.

"He does not do charity work," Henry's mother said, a hint of disgust in her voice. "He does not *do* anything."

"Henry's figuring things out right now," his father quickly explained.

"A gap year," Alan said. "I took one of those between college and medical school. Let's continue with the Seder, shall we?"

"It is not a gap year," Henry's mother said, her accent becoming more and more pronounced.

Henry did not look at his mother. He wouldn't. He couldn't

look at her. This was happening with increasing frequency as of late.

"Let's just give the boy some space, all right, Ursella?" Edmond said. "And we don't have to discuss this here."

"He is not boy," she said. "He is man."

Everyone was sitting up in their seats, watching this unfold. Sarah could see Sylvia's mind racing, thinking of ways to quash this—to bring it back to the elevated holiday meal it had been before all this Henry talk began. Sarah looked at Becca, but she was still looking at Henry.

"Ursella—" Edmond said, only to get cut off.

The doorbell rang, seemingly on cue.

Elijah showed up after all.

The third question:

On all other nights, we don't dip our food even once,
and on this night we dip twice.

Thirty-Three

And there he was. Standing right there, at the Gold family front door.

"Look who's here!" Sylvia cried out, throwing her arms around him.

Sarah joined the crowd to catch a glimpse of the prophet in the entryway, he whose presence signals the coming of the Messiah.

Gideon was home.

"I didn't know you were coming!" Sylvia cried, clutching her son as if he were a dream that might slip away. "You should have told us!"

"I wanted it to be a surprise," he said, moving past her to hug Alan, and then Sarah, and then Becca.

Everything about him looked overgrown. His hair was too long, his beard unshaven. Even his fingernails looked like they could use a good snipping. But Gideon looked extra handsome when he was scruffy like this, and he knew the effect it had on the ladies. Sarah wondered if there were any ladies out in Sri Lanka working for Doctors Without Borders. She didn't have to think about it for long.

As Gideon made his way inside, he beckoned beyond the door to a woman who was waiting to be invited in.

"Everyone," Gideon announced, "this is Malika." And then after a suitable pause he added, "My fiancée."

The group erupted into cheers and calls of "*Mazel tov.*" Gideon and Malika were enveloped in warm hugs.

"Wow," Sarah whispered to Joe. "It's going to be a double wedding, just like the Brady girls."

"Be nice," Joe whispered back.

"That *was* me being nice."

No one said the obvious—like that Gideon had shown up without telling anyone. Or that Gideon was engaged and hadn't told his family. Or (and this was the part that Sarah thought would stop Sylvia in her tracks) that Malika was black.

"Do you speak English?" Valentina asked Malika slowly and loudly.

"Well, yes, I should hope so!" Malika replied in a thick English accent. "It would be pretty hard to get around London if I didn't!"

"A Brit!" Valentina said, flipping her hand back as if she were Vinnie Barbarino. "Very fancy."

"Have you started the Seder yet?" Gideon asked. "We were supposed to get in this afternoon, but our flights were delayed."

"Not really," Alan said. "And we'd be delighted to start it over now that you're here."

"Should I call the warden?" Valentina asked.

"Warden?" Gideon said.

"I think I need to lie down for a minute," Sylvia said, and then slipped out of the room.

●   ●   ●

There was just something about Gideon. It wasn't the way he walked, or the way he spoke, or the way he carried himself. It was all of those things put together; the sum of his parts. He was considered classically handsome by most, with his chiseled face and his thick brown hair. Tall, dark, and handsome. Like a 1950s movie star. He paid very little attention to his appearance. He would go weeks without shaving, without having his hair cut, and there was something about this apathy that made women go wild. The way women felt about him was inversely related to how he felt about them. The less he cared about a woman, the more she went crazy for him. It was almost as if he'd planned it that way. But the truth was, he never really cared that much about any of them. Not since the first one that had broken his heart.

And now here he was, engaged to be married. There was something in his face, a softness Sarah detected that had never been there before, that made her think this one could actually stick. Forget about the ring on Malika's finger. It was the look on Gideon's face that told Sarah that this girl could actually be The One.

Malika, of course, wasn't a girl. She was a woman. A grown woman who had gone through just as much training as Gideon to become a doctor, a woman who had seen just as many awful things in Sri Lanka as Gideon, a woman who was hoping to join Sarah's family. And she had a soft face, a kind face. It was the sort of face you wanted to tell all of your secrets to.

•   •   •

Malika wore her hair in a tight bun. There was no electricity in the tents at their base camp, so she couldn't iron her hair out straight, the way she would normally do if she were meeting the family of a white boyfriend. And she thought Gideon would find her frivolous if she'd insisted on stopping at a hair salon on the way (were there any black hair salons in the suburbs of Connecticut?), or if she'd tried to primp in the airport bathroom once they'd landed. Plus, Gideon had told her that his family wasn't like that. They were the serious type, the sort who didn't care about appearances. But now, looking at his sister, with her getup straight out of the pages of a fashion magazine, she knew Gideon had been wrong.

Malika felt uncomfortable. The Gideon she knew didn't live like this. The house was big. Too big. She could barely see it from the street, from the driveway even, where it was concealed by thirty-foot pine trees, but now, stepping into the foyer, she had the sense that everything she knew about Gideon was wrong.

It wasn't the Italian marble that covered the floor of the foyer, or the enormous Hermès vase sitting atop a Louis XIV table that worried Malika. The entryway was beautiful—a perfect circle encased in a subtle tone-on-tone chinoiserie pattern. And it wasn't Gideon's parents that bothered Malika, either. Gideon's mother was lovely. She smiled broadly at Malika when introduced, and didn't seem to flinch when she saw that her son was with a black woman, the way that other mothers had in the past. Her face stayed perfectly frozen, smile in place, as she gently hugged Malika and welcomed her to the family. Gideon's father was more warm-blooded, and just as welcoming. He threw out his arms to embrace Malika, which she wasn't expecting, so her face became buried in his dress shirt. If she'd been wearing lipstick, it would have left a stain on his navy tie.

None of these things bothered Malika. But something *was* bothering her. It was that Gideon's family was exactly like her own. She'd been trying to escape her childhood for as long as she could remember. It had begun at boarding school, where she hoped that her dark skin would help her to blend in with the scholarship kids. (It did not.) It continued at Brown, where she tried to fit in with the dreadlocked black-power bunch. (She did not.) By the time she hit medical school, she'd given up on pretending that she wasn't a rich, privileged brat (though a rich, privileged brat who worked hard and earned everything she had gotten). That was when she discovered Doctors Without Borders. At last, she could do something meaningful with her life, something no one else was doing. Back home, her mother planned charity balls simply for the outfits she could don. Her sister was presently starring in—of all things!—a reality television show about the rich socialites of the London party scene. Malika had found her calling, had found her people, and in Gideon, had found her future.

Or so she hoped. As she shook hands with the various party guests, she couldn't focus. As they made their way into the living room, all Malika could think was that she hadn't registered even one of their names.

•   •   •

Valentina fawned all over Malika, asking her if she knew Elton John, and how she'd met Gideon, and what sort of work she was doing in Sri Lanka. Sarah considered intervening, but instead chugged another glass of wine. If Valentina asked to touch Malika's hair, she vowed to just lie down and die right there in that very house.

"You know what this means, right?" Sarah said to Joe.

"What what means?"

"Malika and Gid," she said. And then, in a barely audible whisper: "She's black."

"I noticed," he whispered back.

"So," Sarah whispered. "That means, we're winning! I mean, you may not be Jewish, but Italian's got to be preferable to black. After all, you could always pretend to be Jewish, but there's no way a black person could possibly be Jewish."

"This is all sorts of offensive," Joe said, dropping the pretense of whispering. "You do realize that, right?"

"I'm joking!" Sarah said.

"No," he said. "You're not. And I really don't like where this conversation is headed."

"Wouldn't you like it if my parents finally approved of our relationship?"

"I don't really care what your parents think of us," Joe said. "But I know that you would."

He got up and walked to the kitchen, muttering something about needing a drink. Sarah considered chasing him, but the wine had gone to her head. She sat back down on the couch. Becca perched next to her.

"Well, this Malika thing certainly takes the heat off my younger-unemployed-boy thing, huh?"

"Yeah," Sarah said, her eyes following Joe as he walked into the kitchen.

"Chef Michael's pretty cute," Becca said.

"I don't think you're allowed to hit on other men while you're introducing your family to your boyfriend's family."

"I don't mean for me," she said, looking over at the kitchen. "I mean for you. Is he Jewish?"

"I have no idea. How would I know? Anyway, I live with Joe, in case you've forgotten."

"I didn't forget," she said.

"What's the deal with Henry?" Sarah asked.

"What can I say?" she said. "We met at this bar one afternoon and we just hit it off."

"You were in a bar in the middle of the afternoon?"

"It was almost evening," Becca said.

"What do you have in common with him?" Sarah asked. "He doesn't go to school, he doesn't work. You've spent your life going to school and then working your butt off over summers and on breaks."

"That reminds me, I was accepted to this research position for the summer at Yale," she said. "So we'll be able to hang out all the time if I take it."

"*If* you take it?" Sarah said. "I thought you already did."

"Yes, right, *if*," she said. "So, Henry. What can I say? I really like him. He's unlike anyone I've ever met before."

"How so?"

"He's more laid back," she said.

"He doesn't work," Sarah said, laughing. "He doesn't even go to school. If I didn't have anything to do all day, I'd be pretty laid back, too."

"I hate when you get judgmental like this," she said. "Just like Mom."

The biggest insult a person could give Sarah was a comparison to Sylvia. Sarah would rather be accused of murdering puppies than being like her mother.

Becca knew this.

Thirty-Four

Sylvia regained her composure and made her way out to the living room, Gideon following closely on her heels.

"Let's get back to it, shall we?" she announced. She was smiling, pretending that this whole mess wasn't bothering her. Not the unexpected guests, not the fact that her son had come with his black fiancée, not that control of this dinner party was slowly slipping away from her.

Becca and Sarah went into the kitchen with their mother. Three people to get two place settings.

"Where do you want them?" Becca asked, looking at Sylvia's seating chart.

"Let me help you," Chef Michael said to Sarah. Sarah was suspicious. Had Becca told him that this was a fix-up? Had he not noticed that she was here with someone? Someone who worked with metal and tools and grease for a living, not tiny potatoes and cinnamon and apples?

"Put them across from your sister," Sylvia said, as if Sarah were not even there.

Sylvia walked to the stove top and stirred the matzoh ball

soup. Chef Michael may have taken over cooking duties, but it was still her kitchen.

"You need an oven mitt," Chef Michael cautioned Sylvia, but it was too late. She hadn't realized the ladle had been left in the pot of soup, and was roughly the same temperature as the soup. Which is to say, scalding.

Sylvia recoiled in pain.

"Let me put butter on that for you," Sarah said.

"That's the exact opposite of what you should do," Becca said. "Let's get it under cold water." She held Sylvia's hand as they walked together to the sink. Relief washed over Sylvia's face as the cool water from the faucet ran over her hand.

"Thank you, Becca," she said. She tried to remove her hand from the sink, but Becca held firm.

"Five to ten minutes, Mom," she said. "You're blistering a little."

"I'll get some ice," Sarah said. "Maybe that'll speed things up."

"She can't put her hand directly onto ice," Becca said. "It could stick to the burn and make things worse."

Sarah saw she was not needed; she quietly left the kitchen.

The seating cards were all for naught. Gideon and Malika had already made themselves comfortable on opposite sides of the table, each next to a Rothschild. That Gideon and Malika would sandwich themselves between the hosts and the Rothschilds, that they would completely upend her plan that her guests of honor would be seated next to their hosts in seats of honor . . . well, there were no words.

"I know that you like to split the couples up to encourage conversation, Mom," Gideon said, smiling. He was expecting his gold star now.

"Yes, honey," Sylvia said, and sat down in her seat. Becca had applied bacitracin to her hand and had bandaged it for her. She skipped the ibuprofen Becca had suggested in favor of another glass of wine.

"What happened?" Alan rushed to Sylvia's side.

"It's nothing, honey," Sylvia said. "Becca came to my rescue."

Alan examined the gauze, turning Sylvia's hand over, and then looked to Becca and said: "Good."

"I could have done that," Gideon said. "Let me see."

"It's perfectly fine," Sylvia said, motioning him to sit back down in his chair. "Let's just get back to the Seder, shall we?"

The Seder reconvened, and Alan let each person at the table read a passage.

"In my family," Malika said, "we usually conduct the Seders completely in Hebrew. Would you mind if I read my part in Hebrew?"

It was Valentina who said exactly what everyone was thinking: "You can read Hebrew?"

Gideon and Malika laughed. *Oh, how funny, you country mouse! Don't you know that black people everywhere read Hebrew?*

"What's so funny?" Sarah asked Gideon.

"Malika's Jewish," he said.

"Oh," Sarah said. "Of course she is. Would you please excuse me for a moment? I'm just going to use the ladies' room. But please, continue."

Sarah got up from the table, ready to use one of her old tricks from middle school. When about to cry at the cafeteria table, it is much better to do so in the bathroom. You can cry in peace, and most of the time, no one will disturb you. No one even has to know.

She closed the door to the powder room and sat down on the floor.

Of course Gideon brought home a fiancée. And of course, she's Jewish. So, he's still winning. He's got a gorgeous fiancée who is Jewish and a doctor, no less. How is this fair? He's supposed to be across the world somewhere. Instead, he's here. Ruining the whole night.

Sarah hated that her brother could do this to her. She hated that this was the way he made her feel. With only Becca around, Sarah could play the role of big sister: advice giver, knowledgeable one, sibling-in-charge. But with Gideon back, it threw everything out of whack. Sarah lost her place, and with it, her equilibrium.

There was a gentle knock on the door. Sarah opened it wide, expecting Joe. "You okay in here, kitten?" Alan asked.

"Those 'deconstructed' potato pancakes disagreed with me," Sarah said. Food poisoning was a hard sell, but it was her only play.

"Crazy night so far, huh?"

"Yeah," Sarah said. "Crazy."

"Do you want me to switch the seating so you can sit next to Malika and get to know her a bit better?"

"No." Sarah knew that she was acting like a teenager, doling out one-word answers with a puss on her face, but she couldn't help it. She felt like she was in high school again, with Joe by her side and Gideon dating the prom queen. Sylvia fawning all over Gid's date like she was something special and ignoring Joe, who had been there all along.

"Okay," Alan said. "You wanna stay here? Or maybe you'd be more comfortable in your old room?"

"I can't go to my room," Sarah said. "Everyone will know that I'm sulking. In here, I can pretend that stupid Chef Michael gave me food poisoning."

"Those potato pancakes were very off, weren't they?"

Sarah laughed. "They were a *deconstruction*, Dad. Don't you know anything about *elevated* holiday cooking?"

"Okay, kitten," Alan said. "I'll leave you to it."

The door shut quietly behind him and Sarah decided her father was right—she could be sick upstairs in her old room just as easily as in the powder room.

Sarah lay on her old bed and thought of Joe. No surprise there, since the room still had her old bulletin board full of pictures of her and Joe from the homecoming dance. Her varsity letter for tennis was tacked up on the board, along with a card that her best friends had all signed for her seventeenth birthday. And next to that, an old *The O.C.* poster adorned the wall, Ryan Atwood and Seth Cohen smiling broadly back at her.

But the bed. How many hours had she spent lying on this bed with Joe? Always with the door open—Sylvia's house rule. But there was something about those talks they used to have. The sorts of talks you just can't have as adults. Hours upon hours to just sit around and talk. Something they almost never did anymore with their busy lives and a house to take care of and jobs. Back then, Sarah and Joe would sit around and talk about crazy big-picture things: theories on life, what they thought of the world, what they wanted their futures to look like. Their present looked a lot like what they had mapped out back then: Sarah at a magazine, his father's shop for Joe, but still, Sarah felt incredibly nostalgic for those times when anything was possible.

Sarah wished her life now could be as uncomplicated as it had been then. No lies, no secrets. No sneaking around. Well, there was sneaking around back then. Lots of it. But for some reason it felt more innocent. A midnight trip to the lake. A quick drive to get ice cream. A stolen kiss at the window in the middle of the night.

Now that Sarah was older, the lies were bigger, the sneaking around more devious. Why couldn't she just be herself around her family? She couldn't tell them anything, it seemed. Not what she really thought of this Passover Seder. Not how she felt about the Rothschilds being invited to a holiday when Joe's parents had never been included for all these years. Sarah couldn't even tell them that she no longer shared a last name with them.

That she and Joe were married.

Thirty-Five

"Where is Sarah?" Sylvia asked.

"She wasn't feeling very well," Alan said. Sylvia knew by her husband's tone that there was more to the story. "Anyway, it's your turn to read, Sylvia. Top of page nineteen."

"Yes, of course. Where were we?" she asked. Truth was, she couldn't see what she was reading very well since she refused to wear her reading glasses in front of the Rothschilds. But she'd been attending Seders her entire life. Surely she could remember.

"Let my people go," Gideon said.

"What's that?" Sylvia asked, thumbing through her Haggadah. She had completely lost her place.

"Moses told Pharaoh: Let my people go! But, as you may recall, Pharaoh said _no_," Gideon said.

"I think he's trying to tell you that we're up to the ten plagues now," Malika offered.

"I'm just going to check on Sarah," Sylvia said, excusing herself from the table. She stopped in the kitchen to check on the dinner. Gideon followed.

"So, I guess I kind of sprung all this on you, Mom." He opened the oven and took out a piece of brisket.

"You could say that," Sylvia responded. "Really, Gideon, a surprise is one thing. A bombshell, another."

"So Malika is a bombshell?"

"No, I'm not saying that. It's just that—"

"It's just what?"

"Nothing, Gideon. She seems lovely," Sylvia said. "Just lovely." Sylvia watched Gideon stuff the entire piece of brisket into his mouth, pushing it in with his fingers. *Does living in Sri Lanka force a person to lose all of his manners and behave like a wild animal?*

"Lovely?" Gideon asked, his mouth full of brisket.

"I was just surprised, is all. I've never met this girl before, never heard her name even once, and now you're engaged to her. Wouldn't you find that surprising if you were me?"

Gideon continued popping food into his mouth. "Is it because she's black?"

At that very moment, Chef Michael lost control of the five-pound bag of ice he was handling and spilled it all over the island, all over the porcelain tile floor, and right onto Sylvia's shoes.

"I'm so sorry," Chef Michael said. "I don't know what happened."

Gideon bent down to help clean up, but Chef Michael insisted he had it all under control.

"Is it because she's black?" he asked Chef Michael. Gideon smiled at his mother. Sylvia did not smile back.

"What?" Chef Michael asked, flustered. He gathered ice up into his chef's apron and put it into the sink. "What do you mean? I wasn't even listening."

"How dare you?" Sylvia said. "I marched with Dr. Martin Luther King, I'll have you know."

"Just because you participated in the civil rights movement doesn't mean you're not a racist."

"That's exactly what it means, in fact," Sylvia said.

"I'm sorry if I've shocked you with Malika," Gideon said.

"Is that why you've brought this woman home? To shock me?"

"I brought her home because I'm in love with her," Gideon said. "She's smart and she's beautiful and she's the only thing helping me keep my sanity over there. I don't know what I'd do without her."

"Then, that's wonderful."

"So, the fact that she's black doesn't shock you?"

"Oh for goodness' sake, Gideon. Give me some credit. It doesn't shock me."

"Good. So glad to hear that it doesn't matter."

"I didn't say it didn't matter. It does. It's a hard world out there and—"

"No. You do not get to do that. Not the 'hard world' lecture. I know how hard the world is. I know what it's like. And I know what you're like, too."

"Gideon," Sylvia said. "I'm frightened for you." Sylvia appeared to soften. Gideon knew better. Still, he saw an opening and he took it.

"Oh, Mom," he said. "You're frightened for an interracial couple?"

He took her hand. She took it back.

"Yes," she said, regaining her steam. "I'm afraid for an interracial couple."

"Are you kidding me? It's been a long time since you marched on Washington. We've come a long way. We have a black president, for goodness' sake."

"Okay, so we have a black president. Just ask him what that's been like. Even Oprah said—"

"Yes, I read that article, too," Gideon interrupted. "'The level of disrespect experienced by this president—'"

It was Sylvia's turn to interrupt. "Disrespect is just where it starts. Don't you know what this means? It means that when the two of you are together, people will say horrible things just because you are white and she is black. It means that my future grandchildren will be hated simply for the color of their skin. It means that my future grandson can be shot down in the middle of the street for no reason other than the fact that he's wearing a hoodie."

"That's a horrible thing to say," Gideon said.

"That's the world we live in," she said.

"So, I shouldn't be with her because we live in a terrible, racist world?"

"I didn't say that," Sylvia said. "You asked me if I was shocked. I told you I was scared. And then I explained the reason why. If you love her, you should be with her. Do you love her, Gideon?"

"Sarah loves Joe," Gideon said. "I don't recall ever hearing this attitude as far as Joe is concerned."

Sylvia regarded her son. He'd come into the kitchen for a fight. He very much wanted a fight. Of that much, Sylvia was sure. He wouldn't leave, it seemed, until she gave him one.

"Do you know how many Jews died in the Holocaust?" Sylvia asked. She walked toward the kitchen table on tippy toes, careful not to disturb the ice, and sat down. Gideon joined her. He didn't walk carefully through the ice. He stormed through it, kicking shards of it this way and that, with Chef Michael following closely on his heels, trying to contain the mess.

"What does that have to do with what I just asked you? About Sarah and Joe?" he asked. Sylvia was seated at the head of the table, in the chair she always sat in, and Gideon sat directly to her right, her willing disciple.

"Do you know?" she asked quietly.

"Six million," Gideon said. And then quickly: "But something like that could never happen today. People wouldn't allow it. The world is different now."

"Why?" Sylvia asked. "Because you think people these days are better? Because you think people actually like Jews? For someone so smart, Gideon, you really have your head in the sand."

"I do not have my head in the sand," Gideon said. "I resent that. You have no idea what I see on a day-to-day basis."

"The man I dated before your father asked to see my horns," Sylvia said. "He was a smart man, a doctor, and he still believed that Jews had horns. I'd find him looking at my head when he thought I couldn't see. Examining it for evidence."

"I don't believe you," he said.

"Fine," she said. "Don't believe me."

"Anyway, things are different now."

"Are they? Have you spoken to anyone at your base camp recently about the Israeli-Palestinian conflict? I bet their views would surprise you."

"You haven't even met the people I work with," Gideon said. "That's quite an assumption."

"You don't see why being Jewish is important?" Sylvia asked. "As the grandchild of Holocaust survivors, you don't see why it's important to be proud to be Jewish, why you should want your children to be Jewish? Why I want my grandchildren to be Jewish?"

"You can be proud to be Jewish and still let your kids be with whoever they want," Gideon said.

"And if that were to happen, in a few generations, there would be no Jews left," Sylvia said. "It's already happening. Conservative synagogues are closing down, they have no membership. No one left to join. Is that what your grandparents escaped Dachau for, do you think?"

"Malika's Jewish," Gideon said.

"Yes, she does appear to be," Sylvia said, cupping Gideon's face in her hand. "Congratulations, Gideon. You're still the Golden Child."

Thirty-Six

Alone on her childhood bed, Sarah could hear her mother's voice in her head, trilling, "They're not married!" But they were. Sarah and Joe had gotten married six months prior, in a small civil ceremony.

They were tired of not having what they'd wanted since they were teenagers: for Sarah to call Joe her husband, for Joe to call Sarah his wife. For the law to recognize what Joe and Sarah had known their entire lives. That they were meant to be together.

The only people they'd told were Joe's parents. As time went on, it was harder and harder to keep the secret. (Especially since Sarah's in-laws weren't what you would call discreet.) And Sarah felt worse and worse about keeping it from her mother. But whenever she ran the scenario through her head, Sarah always came to the same conclusion: if Sylvia could just accept who Sarah was and the choices she'd made, she never would have had to keep it from her from the start.

Sarah knew that Joe was angry about the way she'd reacted to Gideon bringing home Malika. But what he didn't understand was that she was dying to let Sylvia know about her marriage. It killed Sarah every time she saw her, every time they spent a holiday or a birthday together, to know that she was keeping something from her mother. Something huge. The most important thing in a girl's life.

As an only child, there were things Joe just couldn't understand. Like how with three siblings, there was always an odd man out. Always someone to gang up on. The dynamic always changing—sometimes it was Sarah and Becca against Gideon, other times it was Gideon and Sarah against Becca, and sometimes it was Gideon and Sylvia against Becca and Sarah. But they were never united. If pressed, Sarah couldn't remember a single time all three siblings had stood together on something.

Sarah would be lying if she said that she hadn't used it to her advantage over the years. Got together with Becca and Alan to take down Gid and Sylvia, even sided with Gid at times when she knew it would get her her way. Sylvia never took Sarah's side in things. Not the oldest and not the baby. Just in the middle. Easily forgotten.

When Sarah saw Malika, she hoped that she could team up with Sylvia against her, and that would give her the opening to tell Sylvia about her and Joe. That somehow it would be easier to tell Sylvia about her inappropriate spouse if she was upset about her brother's even more inappropriate fiancée. But that didn't pan out. Just another missed opportunity. Another time she could have said something, but didn't.

"The Seder's over," Joe announced as he walked into Sarah's room without even knocking. He plopped himself next to her on the bed. "Is this where we're staying for the rest of the night?"

"I had to get out of there."

"Fine by me," he said. "We can finish what we started earlier." And with that, he rolled on top of Sarah.

"Stop it!" she said, and pushed him back.

"Sorry it didn't work out with the whole black fiancée thing," he said.

"Yeah, that was a tough break," Sarah said.

"You can just tell her, you know," he said quietly. "It doesn't have to be because your brother has made an even worse life choice than you. You can just tell her because you want to."

"You weren't a bad life choice," Sarah said.

"Well, not in your eyes, no," he said.

"You weren't a bad life choice."

"I think we should go back downstairs and join the party," he said.

"Five minutes more," Sarah said.

"Let's go now," he said. "You'll really like it. They're back on Henry now."

Thirty-Seven

"I don't feel like I have to give in to the man like the rest of you," Henry said.

"You were so right," Sarah whispered to Joe. He smiled back. "I wouldn't have wanted to miss this."

"Give in to the man?" Gideon repeated back with a laugh. "Is that what you think I do?"

"All I'm saying is I'm happy where my life's at right now."

"I'd be happy, too, if I could live off Mommy and Daddy's dime," Gideon said to Malika in a stage whisper. She offered an uncomfortable laugh.

"Gideon," Alan said. "That's not how we speak to guests in this house."

"Sorry, Dad," he said.

Valentina sidled up to Joe and Sarah and opened her eyes wide as if to say: *Can you believe this?* Joe shrugged in response and Sarah gave her the big open eyes back. *No! I can't!*

"Nice of you to join us," Sylvia said.

"I think that fake potato pancake made me sick," Sarah said.

"Keep your voice down!" Sylvia chastised.

"No offense," Sarah called in the direction of the kitchen.

"None taken," Chef Michael called back.

"I think it's great if you're happy where your life is right now," Gideon said to Henry.

"Thanks," Henry said. Even though he didn't have a job and didn't go to school, Henry was smart enough to know that Gideon didn't really mean it.

"So what do you do all day?" Valentina asked.

Valentina always said the thing that was on everyone's mind. She wasn't asking to be malicious; she was genuinely curious as to what he did all day. She'd worked her entire life, from the time she was fourteen years old, and the thought of sitting around doing nothing had never occurred to her.

"All sorts of stuff," Henry said. He did not elaborate. "So, what do *you* do all day?" he asked Joe.

"Me?" Joe asked, laughing. How funny that Henry would try to deflect attention from himself by putting it on Joe. "I run my father's shop."

"*Your* shop," Alan and Sarah said in unison.

"Yeah, it's my shop now," Joe explained. "So, I pretty much do everything. Fix cars, run payroll, hire new guys when we need it. And now I'm trying to expand the business into high-end body work."

"You own a small business," the Boyfriend's father said. "I think that's wonderful. Small business is the backbone of our country. You should be really proud of yourself for what you do for your community and the economy."

"We're all very proud of our Joseph," Sylvia said, and for a second Sarah thought she must have misheard her. As far as Sarah knew, Sylvia was not, nor has she ever been, proud of Joe.

But then she crossed the room and stood next to Joe, putting her hand on his shoulder. "So proud."

"You should be," the Boyfriend's father said. "We all should be. It's small business that built this country and it's small business that will save it, too."

"I couldn't agree more," Sylvia said. Her hand did not leave Joe's shoulder. "That's what I always say."

It was not what she always said. It was not something she had ever said.

Sarah formulated a plan: she could take advantage of her mother's showboating for Edmond and announce that she and Joe were married. After all, what could her mother say about it at this point? There she was, standing with her hand on Joe's shoulder, pretending that she adored him, that she approved of him, that she actually liked him. She would not risk looking like a hypocrite in front of the Rothschilds—she'd have to pretend she was happy. Sarah would deal with the fallout the next day.

"Tell them!" Becca said.

I'm about to! Here goes!

Sarah stood up and walked over to Joe. Surely she should be standing with him when she made such a grand announcement? But then something happened. Henry stood up with an announcement of his own.

"I have an idea for a small business," he said. The whole room turned to look at him.

"You do?" his father said. "I'd love to hear it. That's wonderful, son."

"What is this idea?" his mother asked.

"I actually got the idea the last time I was out in Vegas," he said. His father furrowed his brow. "There's nothing guys love more than a good steak. And there are tons of amazing steak houses out there."

"I didn't know you were interested in the hospitality business," his father said, almost under his breath.

"But men also love," Henry continued, "being entertained. I'd say about ninety percent of the men who go to steak houses later go out to strip clubs that very evening."

"That does not sound like an accurate statistic," Joe whispered to Sarah.

"So, I figure," Henry continued, "why not merge the two? Have a high-end steak house—the sort of place that would put Luger's to shame—but have strippers there, too? Genius, right? I can't believe no one's thought of this before."

"Like Hooters?" Valentina asked.

"No," Henry said, barely hiding the repugnance in his voice. "I'm talking about high end. First class all the way. Titanium poles. Costumes by a rotating team of Madison Avenue design houses. Former ballerinas as dancers. We'd start in Vegas, and then launch in the city. Eventually we'll take it out to L.A. What do you think, Dad?"

The room fell silent. Becca looked like she was about to say something—her mouth opened and shut like a fish—but no sound came out. She stood next to Henry, holding his hand.

"Former ballerinas as dancers?" Ursella asked under her breath.

"Titanium stripper poles does sound like first class all the way," Joe whispered to Sarah. She tried to contain her laughter. Even though she felt like Henry was a joke, it didn't seem right to laugh at that moment. It was decidedly unfunny.

"Perhaps we can discuss this later," Edmond finally said, after what seemed like an eternity.

Henry didn't say anything back. He seemed to have been rendered speechless. In fact, everyone seemed to have been rendered utterly speechless.

And then, darkness.

Thirty-Eight

"Is everyone all right?" Alan asked as his guests puzzled over what had happened. (Only later would Alan discover that Chef Michael had plugged in so many small appliances that he caused a breaker to shut off.)

The candles on the table gave off an ethereal glow. Everything looked even more beautiful than before. Sarah imagined what Dominic would have said if he were here: *"Youse all look even more gorgeous all lit up by candlelight!"*

But it was true. The candlelight had a way of bringing out everyone's best features. Making everyone look softer. Blunting the rough edges.

"Well, that certainly was interesting," Sarah said to Becca as they searched their father's study for flashlights.

"That really wasn't his best idea," Becca explained. "He shouldn't have led with that."

"You've heard that plan before?" Sarah asked. She was incredulous that her sister hadn't broken up with Henry on the spot. His idea was dripping with entitlement and sexism, and classism, too. It was the epitome of everything that was wrong with him. Surely her sister could see that? She found a flashlight in her father's desk and focused the beam on Becca's face.

"He has other ideas that are much better," Becca said, shielding her face from the harsh glare of the flashlight.

"Well, they certainly can't be worse than that one," Gideon interrupted. He was holding a humongous flashlight—one of those lanterns that can light up an entire campsite. Sylvia had it stored in the pantry for days like this—they had a tendency to lose power since they were surrounded by so many trees—but Sarah had no idea how Gideon could remember something like that after being away from home for so long.

The girls stared blankly at their brother.

"Nobody asked you," Sarah finally said. She was angry with Gideon. She didn't know exactly why.

"Aren't you happy to see me?" Gideon asked.

"Yeah, nobody asked you," Becca said. She folded her arms across her chest.

"I flew halfway across the globe to see you two," Gideon said. "You'd think you'd be happier to see me."

"I spoke to you four days ago and you didn't tell me you were engaged," Sarah said.

"I spoke to you three days ago and you didn't tell me you were coming home!" Becca said.

"I wanted to surprise you," Gideon said.

"You wanted to shock Mom," Becca said.

"What would shock her?" Gideon asked, his eyes narrowing.

"God, are you just so sick of being the perfect child that you have to rebel?" Sarah asked. "Aren't you too old to rebel at this point?"

"Oh, I'm sorry, Sarah," Gideon said. "We can't all find our inappropriate mates when we're thirteen years old."

"You're only with Malika because she's inappropriate?" Sarah asked. "Interesting." Sarah thought it best not to get into it with Gideon on whether or not Joe was, in fact, an inappropriate mate.

"No," Gideon said carefully. "I'm with Malika because she's brilliant and beautiful and way too good for me, only she hasn't figured that out yet. But I did think it would be fun to boggle Mom's mind a little."

"So, you *are* rebelling now," Sarah said. "Jesus Christ."

"It's not rebelling to find someone you love," Becca said.

"Please don't tell me you think you love that numskull," Gideon said.

"He seems like an ass," Sarah said.

"Hey!" Becca said. "I don't judge your choices. Don't judge mine."

"You judge all of my choices," Sarah said.

"I love him," Becca said.

"He's bringing you down, Becca," Gideon said. "You need to get away from him."

"Get away from who?" Henry asked. He was brandishing a tiny flashlight, one of those pocket flashlights you get for free with a paid magazine subscription.

"This is a private conversation, buddy," Gideon said. "Why don't you go back to Mommy and Daddy and let the adults talk?"

"You don't have to be condescending," Becca said. "I can't stand it when you do that."

"Do what?" Gideon asked. The smirk on his face indicated

that he knew exactly what he was doing. Even in the dark that smirk shone brightly.

"Sylvia wants us all back in the dining room. Dinner is about to be served," Henry said.

"Now you choose to do as you're told?" Gideon asked.

"What, exactly, is your problem with me?" Henry asked.

"Who invited you into this conversation?" Gideon asked. "I'm speaking with my sisters. I'd like for you to give us some privacy."

"She's my girl," Henry said. Sarah looked to Becca to see if that caveman statement had made her cringe. On the contrary: she was smiling.

"She is not your girl," Gideon said. "She's my sister."

"Those two things are not mutually exclusive," Becca said. She took Henry's hand and left the study.

Thirty-Nine

"This girl," Edmond whispered. "He needs her."

"You think I don't know that?" Ursella said, turning to her husband. She looked so beautiful in the candlelight. No different than when they'd met, more than twenty years ago.

"Of course you do, sweetheart," Edmond agreed. "But he needs to formalize things. He needs to move forward with a—"

"Formalize?"

"He needs a wedding."

"No, dear . . . not a wedding. That's going too far, too fast."

Edmond knew how this must look to Ursella, how his appeals for a wedding for their son seemed premature, pushy even. He knew, too, that fathers weren't supposed to be the ones who thought of these things. But he wanted his son to establish himself. And he wanted a diversion.

What Ursella didn't know, what Edmond hadn't yet told her, was that he was keeping a secret. Something he couldn't tell anyone. The bank was in trouble. The Rothschild World Bank. The business that his family had started in the 1800s, and then rebuilt after World War II, was collapsing. And he didn't know what to do about it. It wasn't his fault—not entirely—but he would be the one to take the blame. He had spent months trying to figure out some way, any way, to dig the bank, his family's legacy, out of the enormous hole they'd put themselves in.

But now he was out of ideas. The bank was collapsing and there was nothing anyone could do about it.

Earlier, in Becca's room, Edmond had looked out at the backyard, with its green, green grass, and flat plains—perfect for a tent—and realized that what he needed was a wedding. A good influence on Henry wasn't enough. What Edmond needed was a distraction. Something to salvage the two-hundred-year-old legacy of the Rothschild name. And a wedding was the perfect thing.

It was the Rothschild way.

It had all started in 1920, when Joseph Rothschild discovered that his apple- and grape-importing business was being investigated for possible prohibition violations (true). He arranged for his son to marry the daughter of a senator, a close personal friend of the family (on the payroll of the family). The wedding was attended by all of high society, as well as other like-minded politicians whose loyalties could easily be swayed. No alcohol was served at the nuptials. The charges were dropped.

Then, in 1949, when George Rothschild was accused of being a Communist (he wasn't, he was gay), the Rothschild family threw the biggest wedding Los Angeles had ever seen. He married Lana Sterling, an up-and-coming starlet who was more than happy for the column inches in the society pages and gossip rags alike. George avoided the Hollywood blacklist and his young bride signed a five-year contract with Paramount.

Even Edmond's own marriage to Ursella was a direct result of the Savings and Loan scandal of the 1980s and '90s. The engagement was not—he had wanted to propose the first night he laid eyes on her, it was his mother who had encouraged him to wait the three months before presenting Ursella with a ring— but the hastened wedding date was. There were whispers in society circles of an unexpected pregnancy (untrue), but Edmond didn't care about the rumors. All he cared about was calling Ursella his wife. And all his father cared about was keeping the Rothschild name away from the newspapers, away from the prosecutors. And the plan worked. The Rothschild family name was never associated with the S&L scandal, any and all mentions were of Ursella and her "predicament." When it became clear that Ursella was not in the family way, the focus shifted to her charity work, which pleased Edmond's father to no end.

And the Golds were just as good as any other family for an attention-diverting society wedding, weren't they? The girl's father was a doctor, for God's sake. A heart doctor. A man who fixed *children's* hearts. Edmond couldn't have planned it better if he'd tried.

He could picture it: a giant tent set up in the center of this two-acre backyard (Edmond remembered that detail from the tour), the bridesmaids milling around, the groomsmen handsome in their white dinner jackets, and the bride—a good girl from a good Connecticut family, on her way to becoming a doctor. Becca would glide down the grand staircase in the Golds' entryway in a beautiful gown with white gloves (were gloves too much?) and her blond hair fanning out behind her. That would be the image they'd print on the front page of the Style section.

And he could picture the Vows column in the *Times*:

Rebecca Leah Gold and Henry William Rothschild were married on Saturday evening at the bride's childhood home in Connecticut.

A massive sailcloth tent hosted three hundred guests, all close friends and family. A six-course tasting menu featured salads crafted from the romaine lettuce produced by the groom's family, and wine pairings from Château Lafite Rothschild. The guests danced under the stars to the music of a fourteen-piece orchestra.

"I could not think of a more perfect woman to help carry on the proud tradition of our family name," the groom's mother, Mrs. Ursella Rothschild, former principal dancer in the Kirov Ballet in Leningrad, said of the bride.

"She always wanted to help people," the bride's father, Dr. Alan Gold, Director of Pediatric Cardiology at Connecticut Children's Hospital, said of his daughter.

The bride and groom met—of all places!—in a bar near Columbia University, where the bride is studying medicine.

"I knew right away that Becca was someone special," the groom said. "After all, I always listened to my father when he taught me about the markets. Specifically, the value of gold."

"Well, we need to do something," Edmond said.

"*We* don't need to do anything. *He* needs to do something.

Going back to school would be a good start," Ursella said. "Why don't you tell him that you'll back his silly business proposition, but with one condition: that he return to university in the fall and graduate with a degree in business?"

It was a good idea, Edmond had to admit. A great one, in fact. But it wasn't enough to help his current predicament.

"There usually isn't this much excitement at a Gold family holiday," Sylvia said as she emerged breathless from the kitchen.

"Everything is lovely, Sylvia," Ursella said, grasping Sylvia's hands in hers. Edmond, in that moment, could see that Ursella had her. Sylvia was completely taken with his wife. It wasn't difficult to fall in love with Ursella. Everyone always did.

"Mrs. Gold," Chef Michael said. "Would you like to do a tasting before dinner is served?"

"Won't you excuse me?" Sylvia said, and went back off into the darkness, toward the kitchen.

"He needs a wedding," Edmond repeated.

"Don't be ridiculous," Ursella said. "It's too soon."

Edmond and Ursella had become engaged three months to the day from their first date; Edmond didn't see why Henry had to wait any longer. He told his wife so.

"When you proposed to me, you were already running your father's bank, and had been for some years. You were a man. You supported your entire family. Our son can't even support himself. He hasn't graduated college. He hasn't even figured out why it's important that he should."

Ursella was laughing as she said this.

"We need this," Edmond said.

"You look so worried," Ursella said, rubbing the lines in Edmond's forehead. She leaned over to kiss his head. Edmond's hand went up to where Ursella had kissed him, almost on instinct.

"Why do you look so surprised that I kissed you?"

Forty

"Hey, do you remember this?" Sarah was holding up Joe's old letterman jacket.

"Of course I do," Joe said with a smile. Joe had played football in high school primarily so that he could get that letterman jacket to give to Sarah. He felt a little sad that it had ended up in Sylvia Gold's basement. "You used to look so cute wearing it around school. You should bring it home and start wearing it again."

Sarah giggled. Something about being down in the basement with Joe, lit only by a Maglite flashlight, was making her giddy. And, the wine.

"Careful!" Joe called out, but it was too late. Sarah tripped over a set of luggage. "Are you all right?"

"No," Sarah said. Joe rushed to her side. He pressed his lips to her cheek and felt a tear running down her face.

"Where are you hurt?" Joe flashed the light along her legs—was something broken?—and then her arms, and then up to her face.

"I just bumped my knee, I think," Sarah said.

"Should I call for a doctor?" Joe asked, his hand on her knee. "There are a bunch of them upstairs."

Sarah laughed a big hearty laugh.

"No," she said. "Let's just get the lights back on."

"You're still upset?" It wasn't really a question. Joe knew the tears streaming down her cheek weren't because of her bumped knee.

"No, I'm fine," Sarah said, as he helped her to her feet.

"That's good," Joe said, and used the flashlight to illuminate the path to the boiler room.

"What on earth is this?" Sarah asked, as they came upon a clothing rack, filled with various castoffs. Most of the clothing looked old-fashioned to Joe, but what did he know? "I'm taking this," she said, removing a mink vest from its hanger.

"I was just saying that we don't get attacked by animal activists often enough. You should definitely take that. Red paint would look good on it."

"I think that if it's vintage, you're okay. I mean, the vest is already here. It's not like we killed any new animals to make it."

"Does it have a tag that reads: 'It's okay, everyone! No new animals killed—just really old ones. And they probably died of natural causes.'?"

"You don't like it?" Sarah asked, draping it onto her body and then doing a spin for Joe.

"No, I don't," he said. "It's too 1970s. Too *Starsky and Hutch*."

"It's not *Starsky and Hutch*," Sarah said. "It's Bianca Jagger."

"Who's that?" Joe asked and Sarah pretended not to hear.

"It's so old it's actually new again," Sarah said, looking around for a mirror. She took the flashlight from Joe and scanned the basement for a reflective surface.

"Let's just go flip the breaker and see if that works," Joe said.

"You can try on your mother's old musty clothing once we have some light."

"Admit I look good," Sarah said. He could tell her sadness was lifting. And that she was drunk. She was walking like a runway model now, cocking her hips and swinging her arms. "You could say a lot about my mother, but her style was always on point."

Another memory: Sarah, at a birthday party when she was seven years old. When she sat down to eat her cake, she overheard two of the other mothers talking about Sylvia. Sarah had smiled to herself when she'd realized that the women were talking about her mother's clothing, and how she always dressed so beautifully. But then one said to the other: "But, you're pretty, so you don't need the fancy clothes to make yourself look better." And they had both laughed. Sarah had felt embarrassed, whether for her mother or herself, she didn't know.

"Hey, dance with me," Joe said, wrapping Sarah up in his arms. He ran his hands along the fur. "This thing *is* pretty soft. I think I get it."

Joe and Sarah swayed to no music, their arms wrapped up in each other, Sarah's head pressed to Joe's chest.

"I love you, you know that?" Joe asked Sarah. He kissed the top of Sarah's head.

"Of course I do," she said, looking up at him. "I love you, too."

"Then, why are you still crying?"

Sarah didn't know.

Forty-One

"Where have you been?" Malika asked Gideon. The lantern illuminated everything around them. Malika turned off the small flashlight Alan had given her. She didn't need it as long as she stood next to Gideon.

"Trying to talk some sense into my sister," Gideon said. He took Malika's hand in his and kissed it. She pulled her hand away. "Now you, too?" he asked her. "Is there something in the water here?"

Gideon looked at her; she didn't know what to say. This was how it was with Gideon. When he looked at you in that way, his eyes burning into you, it was hard to speak, let alone tell him something he didn't want to hear.

What she wanted to say, what she should have said, was this: *I've made a mistake. We've both made a mistake. And the sooner we fix it, the less it will hurt.* But Malika couldn't say any of that. Not with her hand in his (he'd pulled it back), not with his eyes burning into her (like they always did), not in the house he'd grown up in (even if it did bear a striking resemblance to the one she'd grown up in).

"I just didn't know where you were," Malika said.

"I was trying to talk some sense into my sister," he said.

"She seems perfectly happy to me," Malika said.

"That's just because you don't really know Becca," Gideon said. "I know her. No way in hell she's happy with that loser."

"She doesn't seem to think he's a loser," Malika observed. She turned Gideon's head to face what she was watching—Becca and Henry kissing chastely by the front door in the dark.

"I have to go break that up before my mother sees them," he said.

Malika pulled him back. "No," she said. "You don't. Your sister seems like she can take care of herself and your mother seems delighted that Henry's family is here."

"I have to do something," Gideon said.

"Then let's go say hello," Malika said. "Offer them some light."

"What do you want?" Henry asked.

"Sorry about earlier, man," Gideon said. His head was down and his eyes didn't meet Henry's. He was only apologizing for Malika's sake.

"Whatever." Henry turned back to Becca. Malika watched as brother and sister had a staring contest. Gideon spoke first, and in Henry's general direction: "Did you know she graduated valedictorian from high school?"

"I did know that," Henry said.

"Did you graduate at the top of your class?" Gideon asked. And then, quickly: "Oh, I'm sorry, I meant: did you graduate high school?"

"Yes, I graduated high school," Henry said.

"Good," Gideon said, "because my sister there is a real catch."

"I know that," Henry said. "We really understand each other."

"How on earth can you understand my sister?" Gideon asked, his cool exterior becoming ruffled. "She graduated college at the top of her class. She's in medical school, for God's sake, and just scored one of the most prestigious internships a first-year can get. Whatever she wants, she gets. How can you possibly understand her?"

"I usually get what I want, too," Henry said. "And maybe your sister doesn't want all that anymore. She may not even do the internship this summer."

"Is that true?" Alan asked, materializing out of nowhere. He held a large lantern that threw off a lot of light, just like the one Gideon was carrying. "Becca, you're not doing the internship?"

"I haven't decided," she said, her voice small.

"That internship is important," Alan said. Standing across from Becca, Alan looked so very large. She felt his presence looming over her, like a cartoon villain casting a shadow over his prey.

Malika had the sudden sense that she shouldn't be witnessing this conversation. She pulled at Gideon's arm—surely dinner must be on the table by now—but he pulled back. He wasn't going anywhere.

"I know it is, Daddy," Becca said, her eyes downcast.

Alan didn't say anything. His eyes burned into her, long and hard. She could feel his eyes on her face, but she wouldn't look up. She couldn't. This was new—disappointing a parent—and she didn't know how to process it.

Then, the lights came back on.

"Dinner," Chef Michael said, "is served."

Forty-Two

Dinner was slightly *elevated.* The brisket wasn't cooked with the recipe that had been passed down from Sylvia's grandmother to Sylvia's mother to Sylvia. Missing was the thick tomato-based sauce that had been the flavor of Sarah's childhood, the taste Sarah tried to achieve when she cooked it herself, but never could. Chef Michael's brisket was served with a red-wine reduction.

There was no sweet potato pie casserole, that gooey and sweet Passover dish topped with melted marshmallows that everyone fought over when it came time for seconds. (No one would be clamoring for seconds this evening.) Chef Michael's sweet potatoes were different. For starters, they weren't served in a casserole dish. Rather, they were scalloped and served stacked, one on top of the other, with a glaze in between each potato slice. Sarah thought she tasted maple, but she couldn't be sure. There were no marshmallows.

Sarah ached for her mother's cooking: gefilte fish (cue the stories of her father's parents making it in their bathtub), matzoh ball soup (which she loved helping her mother make—the secret ingredient in the matzoh balls was the seltzer water), stuffed cabbage (Sarah refused to eat it, but still loved watching her mother meticulously fold each piece). But at Chef Michael's Passover table, there was not a kugel or a farfel or a babka to be found.

There was, however, wine. Sarah helped herself to another glass.

"We're just delighted that Becca is such a good influence on our Henry," Ursella was saying.

Sylvia beamed back at Ursella, while motioning to Sarah to take off the fur vest. Sarah ignored her.

"She's accomplished so much," Edmond chimed in. "We're hoping she'll rub off on Henry a bit." He let out a fake laugh in Henry's direction. Henry pretended not to hear any of it.

"Our Becca really is amazing," Sylvia said. Was she being sincere—did she truly feel that Becca was amazing?—or was this her way of trying to guilt her daughter into taking the internship? Becca couldn't tell. Her father hadn't had time to talk to her mother privately, but still, Sylvia knew everything. Or so it seemed to Becca. "Before we turn around, we'll have another doctor in the family," Alan said, smiling. "Malika, I bet you have a lot of stories to share with Becca."

"I do," Malika said. She then took an enormous bite of brisket, hoping the conversation would turn to someone else.

"It would be wonderful for Becca to have such an accomplished female doctor as her mentor," Alan continued. "I know it seems like it shouldn't matter, but even today it's important for a girl to have a woman in her field to look up to. Someone she can go to for advice."

Malika smiled and took a sip of wine. She didn't know how

to tell Gideon, let alone Alan, that she wouldn't be around long enough to serve as Becca's mentor. She shoveled a huge bite of sweet potatoes into her mouth.

"Where did you go to medical school?" Valentina asked. "England?"

Malika nodded, her mouth still full of food.

"So you can't practice here, then?" Valentina asked.

"She can practice here," Gideon said. "In fact, after we fulfill our obligation to Doctors Without Borders, we plan to get married and live here."

"You do?" Sylvia asked. She clapped her hands together, like a little girl. "How wonderful!"

"Yes, it is," Gideon said. He looked to Malika, who gave him a tight-lipped smile in return.

"I'm delighted that my whole family will be here," Alan said. "And I'm just so happy that Gideon's found Malika, and Becca's found Henry. We are all so very lucky."

"Hear, hear," Sylvia said, and raised her wineglass, as if Alan had just given a toast.

"Hear, hear," Edmond said, and smiled at Ursella.

"Hear, hear," Henry and Gideon said in unison.

Everyone began clanging their wineglasses together, celebrating, smiling. No one seemed to have noticed that Sarah and Joe were left out of the merriment. Except for Sarah. And Joe. And Valentina.

"And that Sarah's found Joe," Valentina said, and raised her glass.

"Yes, of course," Alan said, his glass still in the air. "That Sarah's found Joe. Hear, hear."

"Hear, hear," Edmond said. "Those two have actually been together the longest. How wonderful."

"You know what's so funny, Valentina?" Sylvia said. Sarah couldn't be sure, but was her mother slurring her words?

"What's funny?" Valentina asked.

"Alan and I didn't think they'd last past junior high!" Sylvia joked.

"Sylvia," Alan chastised.

"I'm sure you don't mean that," Ursella said. "Joe is lovely. And what a beautiful couple they make together."

"He is a very impressive young man," Edmond said.

Sylvia sat up a bit straighter in her seat. Sarah could tell that she was about to say something, something about how she was *so proud* of her Joe, like she'd said before, but Valentina spoke before Sylvia had a chance to.

"Well," Valentina said, "I, for one, feel lucky that Sarah is a part of our family now. I wish you felt the same way about our Joey."

"They're not married!" Sylvia trilled. "Not part of the family just yet!"

"I really wish you'd stop saying that," Sarah said.

"Well, I'm just stating a fact, sweetheart," Sylvia said. "I didn't mean any offense by it."

"I just really wish you'd stop saying it," Sarah said again. She put her wineglass down. It was empty. She struggled to recall exactly how many glasses she'd had so far.

"I'm only saying what's true," Sylvia said. "Why is there anything wrong with that?"

"Because we *are* married," Sarah said. She couldn't believe she'd said it. She'd actually said it out loud. She'd imagined this moment so differently—the moment when she told her mother the truth. There wouldn't be a crowd watching them, for one, and she wouldn't be telling her mother out of spite. To get back at her. She'd be telling her so that they could both be happy.

"What do you mean you're married?" Sylvia laughed. "You're not even engaged!"

"I mean that we're married. We went down to the court-house on a Tuesday morning and said our vows and got married. I wore a white dress and everything."

"Did you know about this?" Sylvia asked Alan. But he didn't need to answer. The color drained from his face and his brows furrowed into two very pronounced squiggly lines. "Did *you* know?" she asked Valentina.

Valentina looked at Joe, and then she looked at Sarah. She didn't say a word. In that moment, seeing Valentina speechless, a woman who was never at a loss for words, who never let an opportunity to speak pass her by, Sylvia knew.

Sylvia quietly got up from the table. "Would you all excuse me, please?" Alan followed her out.

All eyes were on Sarah. She didn't know what to do. Hop up from the table and follow her mother out of the dining room? What could she even say to her?

Sarah hadn't meant to hurt her mother, after all.

Or had she?

Dessert was never served.

BOOK THREE

The Clean-Up

The fourth question:
On all other nights we eat sitting or reclining,
and on this night we only recline.

ONE LITTLE GOAT

(Chad Gadya, *translated to* "One Little Goat")

One little goat, one little goat.
that Father bought for two *zuzim*,
one little goat, one little goat.

Then came a cat
and ate the goat,
that Father bought for two *zuzim*,
one little goat, one little goat.

Then came a dog
and bit the cat,
that ate the goat,
that Father bought for two *zuzim*,
one little goat, one little goat.

Then came a stick
and beat the dog,
that bit the cat,
that ate the goat,

that Father bought for two *zuzim*,
one little goat, one little goat.

Then came fire
and burnt the stick,
that beat the dog,
that bit the cat,
that ate the goat,
that Father bought for two *zuzim*,
one little goat, one little goat.

Then came water
and quenched the fire,
that burnt the stick,
that beat the dog,
that bit the cat,
that ate the goat,
that Father bought for two *zuzim*,
one little goat, one little goat.

Then came the ox
and drank the water,
that quenched the fire,
that burnt the stick,
that beat the dog,
that bit the cat,
that ate the goat,
that Father bought for two *zuzim*,
one little goat, one little goat.

Then came the slaughterer
and slaughtered the ox,
that drank the water,
that quenched the fire,
that burnt the stick,
that beat the dog,
that bit the cat,
that ate the goat,
that Father bought for two *zuzim*,
one little goat, one little goat.

Then came the Angel of Death
and killed the slaughterer,
that slaughtered the ox,
that drank the water,
that quenched the fire,
that burnt the stick,
that beat the dog,
that bit the cat,
that ate the goat,
that Father bought for two *zuzim*,
one little goat, one little goat.

Then came the Holy One,
Blessed be He,
and slew the Angel of Death,
that killed the slaughterer,
that slaughtered the ox,
that drank the water,

that quenched the fire,

that burnt the stick,

that beat the dog,

that bit the cat,

that ate the goat,

that Father bought for two *zuzim*,

one little goat, one little goat.

Forty-Three

The bank collapsed on a Sunday. It seemed strange to Edmond that the news of it happening should break on a Sunday. When he took over the bank from his father, gentlemen didn't work on Sundays. They worked during the week, from Monday through Friday. Weekends were reserved for family, for leisure activities. But times had changed. The world had changed.

He was eating his breakfast when he heard the news. *The New York Times* spread out on the kitchen table, Edmond had switched on MSNBC—background noise while he ate his poached eggs, whole wheat toast, and fresh fruit. It was then that he heard the newscaster announce that his bank, the bank that his family had started in the 1800s and then rebuilt after World War II, was going bankrupt.

As the newscaster passed around blame (it was Edmond's fault, it was his CFO's fault, it was Edmond's father's fault), Edmond thought about what he would do next. It seemed to him he'd been trying to fix things at the bank for as long as he could remember (even though it had only been fourteen months) and nothing had worked. He had borrowed money, he had used that money to cover other monies that had been lost, he had gotten new investors in. New executives. Young kids who were supposed to have all the answers. (They did not.) Now, Edmond was out of ideas.

"Is there something you should have told me?" Ursella asked as she walked into the kitchen in her nightgown, covered by a silk kimono.

"Well, yes," Edmond said. "But I could never find the right words. We were worried about Henry and I didn't want to give you anything else to worry about."

"But I worry about you," Ursella said, walking over to Edmond. Then, she did something unexpected. She perched onto his lap and put her arms around his neck. "You should have told me."

"I know," Edmond said. Had he brushed his teeth before coming to eat? Ursella's face was so close to his. "I should have."

"Whatever the trouble is," Ursella said, "we'll be fine."

"Oh, I don't think we'll be fine," Edmond said. "This is the beginning of the end."

"Then we'll start over," Ursella said. "I could always go back to dancing. I had a very promising career at one point, you know."

She got up off Edmond's lap and did a pirouette, the flaps of her kimono flying as she twirled. Edmond remembered the first time he had ever laid eyes on Ursella. A beautiful spinning top. He thought she looked the same now as she had then.

"Beautiful," Edmond said.

"Thank you," she said. "Now it's your turn."

"Oh, I don't think I could twirl like that," Edmond said.

"Not to twirl," Ursella said. "To tell me what's going on."

"What's to tell?" Edmond said. "The bank's going under. I'm a huge failure. Thousands of lives will be affected, and there's nothing I can do about it."

"There has to be something you can do. You always solve every problem. Let's brainstorm what can be done."

"I've been brainstorming for over a year now," Edmond explained. "It's over."

Ursella was silent for a moment. Then: "You've kept this from me for over a year?"

"I thought it best not to involve you in this mess." Edmond rubbed his temples; a dull ache was taking form behind his eyes.

"How could you keep something from me for over a year?" she asked, breathless. In disbelief.

"I don't know," Edmond said. He took a slow sip of his orange juice. "I'm sorry."

"I couldn't keep something from you for over an hour," Ursella said quietly. "A whole year, Edmond?"

"I'm sorry," he said. He couldn't seem to apologize enough. Which was good practice for what was to come; he'd be apologizing quite a lot during the coming year.

"I'm not asking you to apologize," Ursella said. "I suppose I'm trying to figure out how you could have done that. How you could keep a secret from me for so long. What other secrets are between us."

Edmond drew his wife to him. He wrapped his arms around

her silky frame and held tight. Ursella buried her face in Edmond's shoulder and began to quietly cry.

"There's nothing else," Edmond said. "I promise you." But as much as he said that, and as much as he apologized to Ursella, nothing could console her.

Forty-Four

Sylvia and Alan did not take the news well. They somehow felt that Becca's decision to skip her summer internship was an indictment of them. Of the way they'd raised her, of the way their family valued education, of the way the Golds always strove for the best.

"Is it wrong to want you to live out your potential?" Sylvia asked her daughter.

"I need a break," Becca said. That was all she ever said in response to the bevy of questions she'd been subjected to. She felt like a prisoner facing a firing squad, blindfold over her eyes, a cigarette dangling from her lips.

What will you do all summer?

Is this because of Henry?

How will this affect your standing at medical school?

No one dared ask the next question, the question that came after all this, the one you asked after all the rest were answered.

Are you even going back to medical school?

Becca knew the questions were coming. Sometimes she thought she achieved so much just to avoid being asked them. She excelled at life only so that her parents wouldn't bother

her. It was actually easier to be at the top of her class in medical school, at her Ivy League undergrad, and her competitive high school than it was to face the scrutiny of Sylvia and Alan Gold. To face the disappointment.

But that was all over now. Her parents may have insisted that being with Henry had "brought her down," but Becca felt it was quite the opposite. Henry showed her that she could do as she pleased. And she planned to do just that. In fact, this summer she'd be spending a chunk of her Bat Mitzvah money (untouched in a savings account since she was thirteen years old) on a Hamptons summer share with some friends. True, her friends would be in the city working all week and out only on weekends, but that didn't matter to Becca. She'd be spending the summer on the beach.

She'd never had so much time to herself before. Her life had been a relentless cycle of schoolwork, summer job, internship, schoolwork, internship, part-time job, schoolwork. Becca couldn't actually remember the last time she'd had more than two weeks off. More than two weeks to herself. Time to do nothing. Time to relax. To rest. And now she had a whole summer to look forward to.

"What will you do with your time?" her mother asked.

"You'll be bored after three days," her father insisted.

But Becca had big plans to do absolutely nothing for two whole months. She planned to turn boredom into an art form. Maybe she'd take yoga classes on the beach in the mornings. Maybe she'd learn to cook.

Maybe she wouldn't.

Becca didn't want to run anymore. Becca didn't want to work anymore. Becca didn't want to tear the tiny little hairs out of her head, one by one, anymore. It was time to stop. It was time to take a break.

Forty-Five

It was a yes. The best yes he'd ever gotten in his life. It was a community college, true, but that didn't matter. The least-prestigious community college (if there was such a thing) in all of New York State. But that didn't matter, either. What mattered was *yes*. It was a yes. As in, yes, you can come join us. Yes, we will accept you. Yes, you can start over.

Henry knew he should be striving higher, but this was all he could get on his own for the time being. And it felt good. He'd do the two years at community college and then apply to a four-year program. Maybe if he could do well here, he'd erase the stink of what he'd done at Florida. Maybe he'd get a second chance.

He was too excited to wait until the fall. For once in his life, Henry actually wanted to do something. He would be starting classes over the summer. Becca was disappointed—she'd be taking the summer off, but she was the reason he'd decided to go back, so shouldn't she be happy for him? After all, he was doing this for them. For their future. Now that he didn't have his father's money to fall back on, he had to do something for himself. Do something by himself.

"Don't you see?" he had told Becca. "This is my chance to step up. To be a man. To be my own man." She had never seen Henry like this before. So eager. So proud.

Shouldn't she be proud, too? Wasn't that what she wanted? That's what Henry had asked himself as he'd pored over the applications for school. But now that he was in—now that he had gotten in by himself—well, NYC Community College felt like Harvard. And more than that, Henry was slowly realizing that it didn't matter who was proud. Not his parents, not Becca's family, not Becca. What mattered was whether or not he was proud of himself. And he was.

There were a lot of papers. Papers to fill out, papers that told him what books to buy, papers that told him where to live. It was all so deliciously overwhelming. He'd asked Becca to help him with the forms and she had told him that if she'd wanted to fill out forms, she wouldn't have blown off her internship.

So, there he was, papers fanned out in front of him, sitting in a downtown Starbucks just blocks away from NYC Community College.

"You can do all of those online." Henry looked up at the guy who had made the comment. "In fact, they encourage it."

"Thanks, man," Henry replied.

And then, as if he were reading Henry's thoughts, the young man said: "The sticker on your laptop. I go to NYC Comm, too." Henry had covered the Florida bumper sticker with one from his new school.

"I haven't actually started yet," Henry said. "I'm starting this summer."

"I started this past January," the guy said and sat down at

Henry's table. "So far, so good. It was either that or another round
of juvie. Didn't even finish high school before I started. Got my
GED and my first semester of college done all in one shot. Not
bad, right?"

Henry had heard that NYC Comm was like the Island of
Misfit Toys—the place you could go when everywhere else had
said no. Is that what he had to look forward to? The guy intro-
duced himself—his name was Trevor—and rolled up his sleeves.
Henry had no idea why anyone would wear long sleeves in New
York in late May. The humidity was already up to 90 percent.
Trevor slicked his hair back with one hand and revealed a sleeve
of tattoos.

You're not going to fit in here, Henry said to himself. He was
wearing a baby-blue collared shirt and a pair of khaki shorts. The
uncool child on his first day of school.

"Nice ink," Henry said. He'd heard people say that on one of
the reality television shows Becca insisted he watch.

"Thanks, man," Trevor said. "I actually want to get it all removed. Change my image, you know?"

"Yeah," Henry said.

"Who am I kidding?" Trevor said. "A guy like you probably
doesn't have a clue what I'm talking about. You look like you've
got it all together."

"Not exactly," Henry said. He wasn't sure, but he thought
he was on his way to making his first new friend at school.
When he'd been down in Florida, he hadn't really tried to be-
friend any of the kids. He had felt completely above everyone
else. He'd had no idea why he hadn't gotten into an Ivy, like all
of his friends had. He'd had no interest in hanging out with peo-

ple whose parents weren't able to get them into a better school. The irony was lost on him at the time.

But this was Henry's fresh start. And he intended to make something of it. Of himself. Partly for Becca, as his parents had suggested, but also for himself. He'd never done something for himself like that before.

"I doubt that I have it any more together than you do," Henry told Trevor.

"Yeah," Trevor said, and laughed. "You *are* going to NYC Comm, after all."

And then Henry did something he'd never done before. Something he'd never thought of doing. He laughed at himself.

Forty-Six

Gideon could not get the video chat to work. He struggled to recall how he'd done it in the past—he must have chatted with Sarah dozens of times before. Hundreds? But he couldn't seem to figure it out.

Could it be that Sarah had always initiated the talk? No, that couldn't be. He'd always made time for his family.

Hadn't he?

After what seemed like hours, but was probably only about fifteen minutes, they were connected.

"Malika left."

"I thought you were both leaving the program?" Sarah asked. "Wasn't that the plan?"

"No, I mean she *left*," Gideon said, careful to keep his voice down. The workers at the camp may have been doing God's work, but they still enjoyed gossip.

"Without you?"

"Yes, without me," Gideon said, losing patience. "She left the program. She left Sri Lanka. She left me."

"You're not engaged anymore?"

"Keep it down," Gideon chastised.

"*You* called *me*," Sarah said.

"Malika broke off our engagement, and she didn't re-up with the program."

"So, when do you come home?" Sarah asked.

"I'm not coming home," Gideon said. "I committed for another year."

Sarah couldn't fathom why Gideon wouldn't want to get back to real life now that his "time was up." (Her words.) But really, how could she be expected to understand that her brother's time in Sri Lanka wasn't just a commitment to a program? Not anymore, anyway.

Gideon had learned a lot about medicine in his time with Doctors Without Borders. He'd learned less about other cultures. Still less about himself. During his time in Sri Lanka, all he had really learned about was Malika. He had earned an advanced degree in Malika Bellamy. From the moment she stepped into his tent, she had consumed his thoughts. The curve of her lips when she smiled, the way she rubbed her index finger and thumb together when she was concentrating, those adorable glasses she would don to look at medical charts.

How many nights had they spent together at the campfire, staying up until the sun rose, talking about their lives? Their hopes for the future. He'd told her everything about himself, and she him. He'd let her see the real Gideon, the one behind the bravado, the person he really was.

And then she left.

Gideon had thought that he and Malika had shared something. He believed that when he had revealed himself to her, that she had done the same. Apparently not. When she left him, she revealed another side. Things Gideon hadn't known before. About who she was, about who her family was. About who she wanted to be. Why hadn't he known any of this before? How could there have been so much that Malika hadn't told him?

Or perhaps she had told him, but he hadn't been listening.

It was Amanda all over again.

It was freshman year of high school, and Gideon immediately felt the shift. Things were different for him. He was no longer the coolest kid at school, the one the girls all cooed over. He was the lowest of the low. He was a high school freshman. He was a boy.

It didn't matter that he stood over six feet tall; there was something different about the seniors. Those guys were no longer little boys, they were men. And the girls, even the freshman girls who, just a year earlier, had been desperate for some of Gideon's time, wanted nothing to do with him.

But not Amanda. Gideon was paired with her in chemistry—lab partners for the year. She was a sophomore, but that wasn't why he wanted her. She was beautiful and smart and kind. When she looked at you, it was like staring at the sun for too long. Her smile made him feel like it was only for him. When she spoke, he could barely believe his luck. That this glorious creature deigned to speak to him.

He first kissed her after a pop quiz they'd both aced. He found her at her locker, filing her papers away in a folder, and he grabbed her. If he'd given it even a second's thought, he would have chickened out. He had to do it fast. When she kissed him back, Gideon felt as though his feet had left the ground. Once he opened his eyes, he was stunned to find that he was still in the corridor, still at her locker. Surely they'd been transported somewhere else?

They became inseparable.

Gideon wanted to do something special for their three-month anniversary. He knew it was coming up because Amanda had circled the date in glitter pen on the calendar she kept taped to her locker door.

But what to get her? Perfect, perfect Amanda, with her long brown hair and cool blue eyes. No regular gift would do. Not perfume—she smelled like heaven. Not jewelry—no adornment could make her more beautiful. Not chocolate—he wanted something that would last.

He recalled a mention of *The Great Gatsby*. Amanda had spoken of the book before, that much he knew. He took the train into the city for a signed first edition of the book. He walked down to the Village to the antique gallery, a store that specialized in rare books. He found the book. Then the dealer told him the price.

"Is this for you?"

"No," Gideon said. "My girlfriend. She loves *The Great Gatsby*."

The bookseller wrote down the name and the address of the Strand Bookstore. "Go here and pick up a hardcover copy of the book. Then, pretend you're Gatsby and write your girl the most romantic note you can muster. Now, *that's* a good gift."

Gideon did as he was told and walked over to the Strand. He bought the oldest-looking copy of *Gatsby* he could find, and inscribed it:

Dear Amanda, Happy anniversary. You are the love of my
life. I hope this book will show you how much you mean to
me. I love you more than Gatsby loves Daisy.

On the day of their anniversary, Gideon could hardly contain himself. He didn't meet Amanda at her locker before homeroom like he usually did. He came to school early and waited for her bus to arrive.

Amanda looked at the book, then at Gideon. "Why did you buy this for me?"

"I remember you talked about it," he said, smiling. Proud. "I wanted to get you something special."

"I told you that I hated this book," she said. "Gatsby doesn't know the real Daisy at all. She's just a dream. What's romantic about that?"

But Gideon hadn't remembered that part.

Sri Lanka was supposed to be his chance to learn about life. About who he really was.

And it seemed to him that in the year since he'd been there, he'd learned nothing. Nothing at all.

Forty-Seven

Sarah put the conference call on mute.

"It's like these people have never heard of the concept of advertising running the magazine," she said to her assistant.

Her assistant laughed out loud. "I know, right?"

"If we didn't have advertisers, we'd have no magazine."

"No magazine," the girl echoed.

Sarah's assistant was straight out of fashion school. She had been hired in equal parts for her style (impeccable) and her grades (As across the board). Sarah was pleased with the hire. She knew her assistant would be promoted quickly, but she still enjoyed working with someone who was smart and motivated, even if it wouldn't last long. It seemed so many of the people who worked at the magazine enjoyed the perks, but didn't want to do the work.

"Why are we even on this conference call?" Sarah asked.

"You're supposed to be talking sense into them."

"Oh yeah," Sarah said, and then fiddled with the phone to take it off mute.

"I have to agree with John on this," Sarah said. "The advertisers need more involvement in the big spread. I saw a few pieces in their fall collection that would work well."

The art department and the executive editor continued talking as if Sarah hadn't said a word.

Sarah's assistant looked back at her indignantly. *How dare
they?* Sarah shook her head in response. *How dare they, indeed!*

When Sarah was young, her father would bring her along
to the hospital on days he wasn't seeing patients. They'd stop
in town to pick up bagels and coffee for the floor, and then Sarah
would camp out at his conference room table while he did his ad-
ministrative work at his desk. She'd sit and draw with her crayons
for hours, while her father dictated charts, returned patient phone
calls, and met with the staff in his department. Throughout it
all—the patients, the hospital staff, the heavy workload—Sarah's
father maintained his composure. He never yelled. Never even
raised his voice. He didn't have to. Everyone, it seemed, hung on
his every word. When Dr. Gold spoke, you listened.

"No, I don't think that's right," Sarah said, as the art department executive explained that the magazine's biggest advertiser
wouldn't mind being put all the way in the back of the book, in
one of the smaller spreads. "They need to be front and center."

Again, Sarah's comment went unnoticed.

"Excuse me," Sarah said in her most assertive voice. "I was
speaking."

She looked to her assistant, who shrugged her shoulders in
response.

"I feel like I'm not being heard here," Sarah said, as the rest
of the conference call proceeded as if she weren't even there. She
took a deep breath—what was it they said about counting to ten
before getting angry?

She looked out her window. She had earned this office. And

the title. And the assistant. Sarah had started out on summer breaks from college as an intern at the magazine. She'd worked hard, and her hard work was noticed. Immediately after college, she landed a job as an assistant and quickly worked her way up. She was a senior fashion editor. Her opinion mattered.

"If I could add something," Sarah said, before being interrupted again. Apparently she could not.

"Text John's assistant and find out what on earth is going on here," Sarah said to her assistant.

"Hey!" Sarah yelled into the telephone. "Hey! Why *the hell* isn't anyone listening to me?" She involuntarily stomped her foot on the ground. "Why did you put me on this conference call if you weren't going to listen to a damn word I said? Why aren't you listening to me?"

Sarah's assistant gasped.

Had Sarah gone too far? Had she lost her temper with the wrong people? She knew John was her executive editor, but he'd always had her back. Surely he wasn't angry with her? And she was fighting to be heard so that she could agree with everything he was saying, so what was the harm in that?

Sarah's assistant stood up and looked at the telephone. She pointed to the red light, which was blinking furiously. The phone had been on mute the entire time.

Forty-Eight

Valentina started the day at the gourmet market, her favorite one over on Front Street. She'd had the butcher carefully select the meats she'd be cooking that night, and help her get started on her antipasto platter. She'd made the pasta by hand, and the gravy, of course, but she wanted to leave the meat until the last second. She wanted the freshest meats she could get—she wanted the very best for this dinner.

Joe was picking up the wine and Sarah was getting the dessert, but Valentina didn't want to take any chances, so she picked up a bottle of Chianti and a Napoleon cake. She wasn't leaving anything to chance.

From a young age, Valentina had been taught that a woman can show her love through her cooking. She could recall meals from important moments of her life: her aunt's braciola on the day of her First Communion; the gnocchi in pesto with fresh sage her mother made on her wedding day; even the risotto Dominic attempted to cook when they arrived home from their honeymoon. A gummy, tasteless mess that refused to spread, Dominic's attempt at his mother's signature recipe (her mother-in-law's risotto, God rest her soul, was a gift from the heavens); Valentina refused to eat it, but she loved that he had made the effort on her behalf.

She was grating fresh Parmesan when Dominic came through the door.

"C'mere, you!" Dominic bellowed. Valentina rushed toward him. It was only, moments later, when they were already kissing, that Valentina realized she still had her apron on.

"I think something's burning, Ma," Joe said, diverting his eyes from his parents, who were acting like teenagers.

"Let it burn," Dominic said, and kissed Valentina again.

Joe camped out in the living room until Sarah arrived. She made straight for the kitchen to drop off the dessert.

"I wouldn't, if I were you. They're having a conjugal visit in there," Joe said.

Sarah peeked into the kitchen. "It's cute," she said.

"I wouldn't mind a conjugal visit myself," Joe said, taking Sarah in his arms.

"Nice try, tiger." Sarah laughed. "Maybe they didn't hear me come in." She walked to the door, opened it, and then slammed it shut.

"My daughter!" Dominic cried out from the kitchen.

The dinner party was back on track.

"Has your husband told you about what's going on at my shop?" Dominic asked Sarah.

"It's very exciting," Sarah said.

"My shop, Pop," Joe clarified.

"Ah, yes," Dominic said. "Joe's shop. You like how he's getting us certified in everything?"

"I think it's a great idea," Sarah said.

"Of course it's a great idea," Valentina said. "Now all those fancy people with their Mercedes-Benzes and Beemers will take their cars to my Joey."

Sarah smiled as Valentina bragged about Joe. What was that expression? Preaching to the choir?

The conversation went like that for a while, everyone going around the table to praise Joe and how his business was already taking off, without any promotions or advertising, simply through word of mouth.

But, of course, that's all to subsidize the real work he'll be doing—the restoration of old cars.

He's the only one in the tri-state area doing work like this.

Already a huge success!

"I'd like to make a toast," Dominic announced, and then stood. "Time away from home makes a man think. I don't care if it's a night out with the guys, or a vacation, or even a stint in a minimum-security joint. Being away from your family makes you realize just how important your family is.

"I'm a lucky, lucky man. I have the most important thing in the world. And I'm never going to do anything ever again that takes me away. You hear that, Val?"

"I hear you, Nicky," Valentina said.

"To family," Dominic said.

Everybody raised their glasses and clinked them all together. Then, there was hugging, lots of hugging.

"Enough of this!" Valentina said, laughing. "We've got three courses to eat—I hope everyone's hungry!"

"Starving," Dominic said.

"Yeah, starving," Joe said.

Sarah opened her mouth and tried to say something in agreement, and was shocked when she realized that Dominic's toast had made her eyes tear up.

Forty-Nine

"I was wondering if you and Dad wanted to come over for dinner this weekend," Sarah said. Slowly, tentatively. She never could be sure how Sylvia would react.

"You mean dinner with you and your *husband?*" Sylvia said.

Things between mother and daughter had not improved. Gideon's decision to stay in Sri Lanka certainly hadn't made things better. Nor had Becca's decision to decline her internship and spend the summer in the Hamptons with thirty-five of her closest friends.

"Yes," Sarah said, "for dinner with me and my *husband.*"

It hadn't taken Sarah long to realize she liked calling Joe her husband. Liked saying the word, even. She liked letting everyone at work know that she and Joe had made it legal, that they were now man and wife.

Her whole life, she thought, she'd had to watch her words where Sylvia was concerned. Now she would do as she pleased.

But how to repair the relationship?

Her previous dinner invitations had been rebuffed (if only we didn't have plans!), but that didn't stop Sarah from trying. She'd visited her father for lunch at the hospital from time to time, and he seemed to be thawing out, but part of her knew that until she made things right with her mother, her father would never fully be on her side again.

"I'll have to check with your father," Sylvia said. "May I let you know?"

"Yes," Sarah said. "No problem."

Sarah knew they wouldn't be coming. Her parents hadn't been to her home since before the Seder. They'd always been so caught up in the fact that she and Joe were living in sin— surely it made things better to know that they had been married all along?

She picked up the phone to call her father. Maybe if she could get him to agree to a dinner date, they would have to come. As she began to dial the number, her assistant came over the speakerphone. It was time for Sarah's 11 a.m. meeting. Sarah checked her makeup, patted down her dress, and made her way out of her office.

Fifty

"The *nerve* she has," Sylvia said. "Who does she think she is?"

"I don't know," Alan responded. Sylvia could hear the hospital intercom through the phone. She knew that Alan was busy at work, but she didn't care. She needed to rant.

"As if I would go to that house of theirs."

"I think it's nice that she's making some sort of an effort," Alan said. "Maybe we should go?"

"I'm still too angry," Sylvia said.

"I understand," Alan said. "I'm angry, too."

Sylvia couldn't understand why Alan was softening. She just couldn't understand it. Sarah had lied to them. Had made fools of them. Didn't he see that? Not only had she denied them her wedding, she'd invited Valentina and Dominic.

That she could never forgive.

When Sarah was in pre-K, the teachers put on a wedding for their unit on the letter *W*. At the time, Sylvia thought it was so inappropriate, forcing the children to model an adult behavior. But she was the only one. The other mothers all thought these miniature weddings were adorable, and insisted on dressing their children up for the occasion. The boys wore jackets, or tuxedo T-shirts. The girls donned white dresses and wore ribbons in their hair.

When Sylvia got to school on the day of the mass wedding, she found Sarah sitting alone in the corner, crying.

"There aren't enough kids in the class, so Joshua is going to marry Emily first, and *then* marry me," Sarah said, her cheeks wet with tears. "It's not fair."

"Miss Mindy," Sylvia called across the room. "May I have a word?"

"Isn't this wonderful?" Miss Mindy asked. She looked around the decorated room. At the cheap paper flowers she'd put on the tables. At the altar she'd hastily created out of cardboard and construction paper.

"My daughter is hysterical," Sylvia said. "I do not think it's wonderful."

"Sarah can be a bit sensitive," Miss Mindy whispered to Sylvia. "We usually just let her be for a few minutes and then she calms down."

"The way you deal with my sensitive child is to ignore her?" Sylvia asked. She was not whispering. The other mothers turned and stared.

Miss Mindy tried to explain, but Sylvia had already scooped Sarah up in her arms and was marching out of the classroom.

Back at home, Sylvia had her own ideas about teaching Sarah the letter *W*. First, they looked at Sylvia and Alan's wedding album. Sarah marveled at the outfits, how old-fashioned everyone looked. Then, they set out to bake a wedding cake. Sylvia had to make do with what she already had in the house, but still they were able to put together two cakes. One vanilla, the other chocolate. They used two different molds and planned to stack the vanilla cake on top of the chocolate one once they were done.

While the cakes were in the oven, Sylvia took Sarah to the basement, where they unboxed Sylvia's wedding dress. Sarah's eyes widened as she took it all in: the silk chiffon, the delicate lace of the sleeves, the hand-sewn beading on the dropped waist.

"Let's get this on you," Sylvia said. Sarah jumped out of the white eyelet dress she'd been wearing, and stood at attention in her white kneesocks and black patent leather Mary Janes.

It was way too big, of course, but Sylvia still thought her daughter looked like a dream. Sarah spun around in the dress, beaming. She peppered Sylvia with questions about what her wedding would look like.

"How many layers will my cake have?" she asked.

"As many as you want." Sylvia laughed.

"Where will we have the wedding?"

"Wherever you want," Sylvia said, smiling broadly.

"What kind of dress will I get?" Sarah asked. And then quickly: "Can I wear your dress?"

"You can wear it if you want," Sylvia said. "I would love it if you wanted to wear it when you're all grown up. That's why I've saved it all wrapped up like this."

Sarah fingered the wrapping paper. Sylvia would have to bring the dress back to the special dry cleaner to have it preserved properly again, but it was worth it. Sylvia imagined Sarah as a grown-up—would she still wear her hair long? Would she be tall, like her side of the family? Would she still think that the wedding dress was beautiful?

The questions continued, but the answer remained the same:

"Anything you want," Sylvia said. "You can have anything you want, my love."

Sylvia went out to her garden. The gardener took care of most of it for her, but the vines needed extra attention and her gardener didn't have the same patience that she did. Sylvia liked to train the ivy. She enjoyed coaxing it into place. She had taken a class at the local nursery, where she'd learned all about the different varieties of ivy, and how the type of climber being trained determined how it should be attached. Sylvia loved learning how the different plants climbed in different ways. Her favorite was the English ivy—a natural climber that needed no help, except in the beginning. She also loved honeysuckle, a twining vine that only needed a strong support, but very little coaxing to tell it where to go. She adored bougainvillea, with its colorful flowers, but it wasn't a natural climber. And it had thorns.

She found it calming to tie the vines to the trellis, to create a pattern, to make something beautiful. She'd already purchased her pruning shears, and she looked forward to that part of the process, as well. Sylvia had fastened the ivy to her trellis, as she'd been taught. She just needed to wait until the vines naturally adhered themselves. They would then climb up on their own from there.

A therapist had once told Sylvia that gardening was good for relieving stress. Was that why she was out there? Hands filthy with dirt, sun beating down on her scalp.

"Looking good!" the mailman called out to Sylvia from the street.

"Thank you, Don!" Sylvia called back.

"How are the kids?" Don asked.

Sylvia winced. It was a reasonable question, the sort of thing people asked each other all the time, but it was the crux of everything wrong in her life at the moment.

Gideon, her shining star, planned to stay in Sri Lanka for another year.

Becca, the one she could always rely on, was in the process of having a breakdown.

And Sarah. Well, she just couldn't discuss Sarah.

"Kids are all doing great, Don," Sylvia said. "Thank you for asking!"

Fifty-One

Becca could not believe her eyes. It looked nothing like the pictures.

The house was filthy. Sand tracked in everywhere, the couches stained and smelling vaguely of a frat house.

"Hello?" Becca called out. Andy, the guy running the share, was supposed to be meeting her. But no one was home and the doors were unlocked. How could Andy go out and not lock the doors? Anyone could walk in. Anyone at all.

She left her bags by the (unlocked, opened) front door. She kept her shoes on. How could she live in a house that was so dirty she couldn't take her shoes off?

She gave herself a tour.

The master bedroom was right off the entryway. There were no sheets on the stained mattress. Two half-empty wineglasses sat on the nearby nightstand. Becca couldn't resist walking into the master bathroom. It was like her first day of Anatomy when she couldn't look away from the decaying corpse. The bathroom was what you'd expect, given the state of the bedroom. A filthy bathtub, a shower with bathing suits hanging over the shower door, dirty towels strewn across the floor. The toilet seat had been left up. A plunger stood nearby. Becca stayed by the door. She didn't want to get any closer than she already had.

"Hello?" Becca heard a male voice call out. "Anybody here?"

"In here," Becca said. Was it okay that she was giving herself a tour?

"There you are!" Andy said. He was wearing board shorts. No shirt. No shoes. A skinny girl in a teeny tiny bikini trailed behind him.

When Becca had first met Andy, he was wearing a suit and tie. She barely recognized him now, his face all sunburnt, hair made blonder by the sun, feet covered in dried sand. "I see you've been showing yourself around."

"I'm sorry," Becca stammered. "No one was here, I thought it would be okay to look around."

"What's mine is yours," Andy said. "No worries. If you're going to live in a share house all summer, you're going to get used to having people being all over you and your stuff. You might even come to embrace it."

Becca failed to see how she could ever embrace such a thing.

Andy tilted his head to the side as if to say, *follow me.* Becca followed, and Andy gave her the informal tour of the house. There was a (very messy) kitchen, a (very messy) family room, and five (very messy) bedrooms. When her three friends came to stay for the weekends, they'd be sharing the bedroom toward the front of the house, the one over the garage, which was filled with four twin beds, barely any room to walk, and a much-smaller-than-expected closet. They'd be sharing a bathroom with two of the other bedrooms, one set up to house three, and the other one, with bunk beds, set up for five people.

"Did you bring your own sheets?" Andy asked. "You need your own sheets."

Becca had not.

"I can take you to Target later," Andy said.

"They have a Target in the Hamptons?" Becca asked, incredulous.

"Oh," Andy said. "You're right. I think it's actually a Kmart."

"Kmart?"

"And we've got a washer-dryer in the basement," Andy said.

"Okay," Becca eked out, her voice getting smaller by the minute. Sweat was forming on her brow and the small of her back. The house wasn't air-conditioned.

What had she gotten herself into? She was miserable already, and the summer hadn't even started yet. How could she relax like this?

"During the week, you can take the master for yourself," he said. "I'm set up in the garage since I'm staying out here all summer to study for the New York bar exam."

Becca hadn't realized that Andy would be staying out at the house all week, like she would. She hadn't thought to ask. *Fucking lawyers.*

"You didn't even show her the best part," the skinny girl said. Becca had almost forgotten that she was there. Would *she* be staying out at the house all summer, too?

"Oh yeah," Andy said. "Here's the best part."

He walked over to the double doors at the edge of the family room. He opened them with a flourish, but Becca stayed put.

"The backyard," she said, making an attempt at a smile.

He did that head tilt again, beckoning her. She walked toward him, and could see the backyard a bit more clearly. Some outdoor furniture had been set up—a table, some chairs, and two chaise longues.

"Not that," Andy said. "This." He opened the gate to a wooden walkway. "Let's go."

Past the walkway, over the dunes, Becca could see the beach. She took a deep breath and felt the ocean air filling her lungs. The seagulls flew overhead, making music with the crashing waves. They got to the beach and Becca took off her flip-flops. The sand was soft, so incredibly soft, and pure white. The water was bluer than she thought it would be, and for a moment she got stuck staring at the horizon. She was completely lost in the view.

"This is where I'll be camped out all summer," Andy said, pointing to his beach chair and umbrella. "Studying for the bar exam in the sun. We can get you some of this gear for yourself when we hit Kmart later. Unless you wanna go now? I can take you now and then we can pick up some lunch in town."

Becca sat down in the sand. She didn't have a beach chair, didn't have a towel, even. But she didn't care. She sprawled out on the sand and let the sun hit her face. She ran her hands through the sand, then her feet.

"I think I'd like to stay here for a while."

Fifty-Two

Alan did not like it when his girls weren't getting along. It didn't happen often, but when it did, there would be fallout for weeks. There was the fight when Sarah was in the eighth grade—over a strapless dress that horrified Sylvia. That lasted about two weeks.

"I will not allow my daughter to dress like a common whore." Sylvia had said this as casually as if she had said, "Pass the broccoli."

"I'm not a whore," Sarah said back. She had that teenaged way of speaking—loud, entitled, without an ounce of humility. "I just want to look nice at the homecoming dance."

"Exactly my point," Sylvia said. "You're not a common whore. You shouldn't dress like one."

"Alison Jacobs is wearing a strapless dress," Sarah pleaded.

"Well," Sylvia said, as if Sarah had just proven her point for her.

Sarah left the table in a huff. She didn't speak to her mother or father for fourteen days. On the Thursday before the dance, Sylvia casually mentioned that she needed something at the mall and that if Sarah wanted to tag along, she could. Just as casually, Sarah said she would go, but only to "keep her company."

They started at the makeup counter of the department store. Sylvia picked up a jar of moisturizer she didn't need.

"While we're here, I suppose it wouldn't hurt to look at some dresses," Sylvia said.

"If you want," Sarah said.

Sylvia picked up a pink cotton dress with a bib collar and a princess skirt. Sarah shook her head and Sylvia put the dress back. Sarah picked up a fitted red dress with a deep-V neckline and held it up to her body. She looked over at Sylvia, but Sylvia put her head down.

They met in the middle of the rack when they both reached for the same lace dress. The navy was so dark that it almost looked black. It was sleeveless with a boatneck. Sarah thought it would show off her collarbones. Sylvia thought it would hide her daughter's décolletage. It had an A-line skirt, and just the right hem length.

"Maybe you should try this on," her mother said.

"I saw something similar in this month's *Vogue*," Sarah replied. She hated to admit that her sense of style was directly inherited from her mother.

"It might go nicely with my gold earrings," Sylvia offered.

Sarah relented and wore the dress they chose together. Even an "appropriate" dress was better than no new dress at all.

Then there was the blowout over medical school. Or the lack of medical school, to be more accurate.

And now this. Sylvia was speaking to Sarah, but only barely. She still refused to be in the same room as her, still refused to accept any of the invitations her daughter had offered.

"I want to show you something," Sylvia said to Alan. She

was out in the garden—she was constantly in her garden now—and she wanted to show Alan what she was working on.

"You've done more," Alan said, looking at the trellis. The vines were climbing now; Sylvia stood proudly before them, like a child showing off her prize.

"I've been working so hard on it," she said. "Do you see how I've got all of this movement over here?"

"I do."

"Each day, I come out and teach the vines where to go. They climb on their own, of course. I'm just giving them a little help so that they look as good as they possibly can."

"Is that what you're doing?"

"Well, what do you *think* I've been doing out here, Alan?" Sylvia asked. A small nervous giggle escaped from her lips.

"I have no idea what you're doing out here."

"This," Sylvia said, pointing to her handiwork. Alan didn't want to admit it, but it looked great. The ivy was climbing around the trellis in a beautiful pattern, its leaves full and green and lush. It was so perfect it almost looked fake. The garden had never looked better, truly.

"What do you think?" Sylvia asked Alan. She smiled at him and waited. Always waiting for his approval. "Hmm?"

"I think you need to make up with Sarah."

Fifty-Three

Joe never needed an excuse to take one of his cars out for a long drive. He loved to hear the roar of the engine, the sound of tires on road, the radio on full blast. The results of his expert handiwork always made him glow with pride. He loved nothing more than driving around, usually to nowhere, for hours on end. If Sarah was sitting by his side, all the better. Today, however, they had a destination.

Sarah wanted Joe to take a portable GPS with them, but he insisted that he knew how to get to Long Island.

"You really just need the LIE," he explained.

"That's it?" Sarah asked.

"More or less," he said. And more to the point: "It'll ruin the clean lines of the car. You don't stick something like that onto an engineering marvel."

They were taking the 1968 Shelby Cobra convertible, the one that Joe had just finished restoring. Sarah had complained that the car was too small. She was certain some SUV would come and drive right over their engineering marvel.

Becca had insisted that Joe and Sarah stay for the weekend. But when Becca found out that weekend guests weren't one of the privileges of investing your life's fortune in a Hamptons share, she told them to come during the week. It took some doing, what with Sarah's production schedule at the magazine and Joe recently having taken over the shop, but they were able to find a quiet week in July. The plan was to drive out on Monday, after the weekend rush was over, then head back to Connecticut on Friday, before the rush started all over again.

Sarah and Joe weren't able to speak with the top down. Well, they could speak, but with the Shelby Cobra sailing down the highways and parkways and expressways at 70 miles per hour, they couldn't hear a thing.

Joe, true to his word, didn't need a GPS. They arrived at the house two hours after they'd left.

"What a dump," Sarah said. "Is it too late to book a hotel?"

"Be nice," Joe said, laughing.

"That *was* nice," Sarah said. "That was actually the censored version of what I was going to say."

The house was large—very large. And while it didn't look like what you'd expect when conjuring an image of "Hamptons house," it wasn't a dump. It was new construction—cheap construction, that much Joe could tell. But, as he would later point out to Sarah, they weren't buying the house, just staying for a few nights.

"You can't park here," a guy wearing a bathing suit and no shirt said to them. He had come out of a garage that wasn't really a garage at all. He was using it as a bedroom. It was a high school kid's dream setup, only this kid was well past high school. He had the half-naked girl in his bed to prove it.

"We're here for Becca," Joe said.

"Oh, cool, great," the guy said. "Nice to meet you. We can

only have two cars in the driveway, and we've got ours here already, so you'll have to park your car down at the train station for the week."

Joe looked at his Shelby Cobra. His baby. The car he'd treated himself to months earlier when he took over his father's shop, and brought back to life on weekends. Then he looked at the guy. He didn't say a word, he just looked at him. He put his hand on the car.

"I mean," the guy stuttered, "I guess it's okay. I mean, I could always move my car. Or my girl can move hers. No worries, man. No worries."

"No worries," Joe said. Sarah stifled a laugh.

Joe and Sarah walked into the house where Becca was waiting for them.

"You're here!" She practically fell over herself to greet them.

"We're here!" Sarah said.

"I have you guys set up in the master for the week," Becca said, walking, leading them on a tour of the house, "and I'll stay upstairs in my usual weekend room."

Joe could see from across the room that the fitted sheets weren't put on the bed properly; one corner of the dirty mattress peeked out at him. The tile floor looked dingy, badly in need of a mop. And the bathroom? Well, that he couldn't even discuss.

"I cleaned for you!" Becca said, beaming with pride.

"Really?" Sarah said. Becca nodded, but Joe knew that the sisters were having two completely different conversations.

Sarah: *Really? You cleaned? It looks filthy.*

Becca: *Yes, really! I love you so much that I cleaned for you!*

"Well, I'll let you get settled in," Becca said. "We have reservations for dinner in town at eight. I picked up bagels and some salads this morning for lunch. Henry's going to take the train out tomorrow after class and meet us for dinner, so we can barbecue then."

She was speaking as if she'd been held in captivity. As if she hadn't spoken a word to another human being in a month.

"Don't put anything down," Sarah instructed once Becca was out of earshot. "This place is disgusting. We're probably going to get bedbugs or an STD."

"It's not that bad," Joe offered, but his heart wasn't really in it. Even he had to admit the place was filthy. Sarah kept their own home tidy and welcoming. She may have had a punishing work schedule, but their place was always clean. Joe had gone from his mother's house to Sarah's. He was not accustomed to mess.

"Thank goodness we brought our own linens," Sarah said. She began making the bed and Joe grabbed the edge of the sheet to help. Once the bed was made, it was on to the unpacking. Sarah refused to put any clothing in drawers where God-knows-what was lurking. She hung everything in the closet. Even her bras and Joe's boxers.

They changed into bathing suits and met Becca out back.

"This is nice," Sarah said. "Fresh air and all that." She draped a towel over a chaise longue and then passed a towel to Joe.

"But this isn't what you come out here for," Becca said, motioning toward the backyard. "You come out here for this." She opened her arms wide, directing their view to the walkout to the beach.

"This what?" Sarah said, sitting down on the chaise longue.

"You're ruining my big reveal," Becca said.

"I think we're supposed to follow her," Joe said, taking Sarah's hand.

"This," Becca said again, as she led them out to the beach. "*This* is what you come out here for." Every time Becca walked onto the beach, she felt it. That instant sigh, the releasing of any tension she was holding in her shoulders. Just putting her feet into the sand, smelling the salty ocean air, did it to her. It was as if she'd been holding her breath and only then, when she walked onto the beach, could she release it.

Joe and Sarah walked out onto the beach holding hands, as Becca quickly ran ahead. The sound of the waves hit Joe, and he pulled Sarah back toward him and kissed her on the lips.

"Mmm," Sarah said, and Joe patted her on the tush. There were hardly any other people on the beach, but Sarah could still feel her face getting a little red.

They caught up to Becca. She had a little village set up for them: reclining beach chairs, towels, and an umbrella. A beach blanket was set out in front of the chairs, creating the sense of a room. She'd even brought out a cooler with waters, iced teas, and fresh fruit. Sarah sat down in her beach chair and Becca told her to lean back so that she could adjust it for her. Sarah appreciated that Becca had bought the chairs just for them; Joe's still had a price tag attached to it. Joe opened the cooler and handed Sarah her favorite—a half iced tea, half lemonade. He grabbed a bottle of water for himself. Joe realized that Becca had set things up so that the cooler served as a side table when they weren't open.

"Isn't this heavenly?" Becca asked as they settled in.

And even Sarah had to admit, it was.

Fifty-Four

Valentina hated it when Joe went away. He never went away for long—he'd been forbidden to attend sleepaway camp when he was a kid and college was simply never an option. But even on long weekends, she missed him. She would count the hours until he was back. It was as if she could sense it when he crossed the border into and out of Connecticut.

"What's bothering my beautiful girl?" Dominic asked.

"Nothing," Valentina said, attempting a big smile. "Every-thing's fine."

"You don't seem fine," Dominic said. "You seem a little sad. What should we do today to change that?"

"You have to go to the shop," Valentina said. "Aren't you supposed to be holding down the fort for the week while Joe is away?"

"You miss Joe," Dominic said. "Why don't you just say so?"

"That's silly."

"Tell you what," Dominic said. "I'll run over to the shop, just to make sure everything's okay, and you go to the market. Get one of your famous picnics together. Spare no expense—I want the best cheeses, the best meats, the best breads. I'll pick up a bottle of wine on the way home. Just like the old times."

Valentina smiled. It was so wonderful to have Dominic back home. But still, her heart ached for Joe. She had always imagined that she'd have a full house, a house full of children. Like the home she'd grown up in. Like the homes her sisters had. Noisy, full of energy, full of love. The home she'd created for Joe and Dominic was full of love, there was no question about that, but she'd always wanted more. Always imagined more. She thought often about the babies she didn't have, the babies she couldn't maintain in her belly. The babies she wanted so badly.

Better to have one healthy child than a dozen sick ones.

Count your blessings, you have Joe.

Some women can't have any children.

Her mother and sisters always tried to make her feel better about the miscarriages, but it was times like these, when she wasn't alone but *felt* alone, that she longed for those lost babies.

When she got like this, Valentina followed her mother's advice to count her blessings. Her sister Victoria had four beautiful children, two girls and two boys, but her husband ran around behind her back. Her younger sister, Viola, had three girls—how Valentina longed for a girl!—but she had also fought off breast cancer twice. Viola was brave, but the second time was so very difficult, both physically and emotionally. She wouldn't throw away her wigs after the second time. Just in case.

Valentina was blessed with perfect health and a doting husband. She had a healthy, happy son who was married to a lovely girl. Why long for the past? Why wish for things that wouldn't come true? Her mother was right. A woman should count her blessings. Especially when she had so many to be thankful for.

"A picnic sounds perfect, Nicky," she said.

He pulled her close and gave her a kiss, fully on the mouth. Valentina wasn't expecting such a passionate kiss before nine in the morning and it made her giggle.

"I adore you, Val," he said. She loved it when he called her by her childhood nickname. She had asked people to call her Tina after Joe was born because she thought it sounded more grown-up, more mature. She had wanted a new name to go with her new life. She wanted to be known as Joe's mother and Dom's wife, not just one of the Ambrusio girls: Vic, Val, and Vi. So Tina it was. But when Dominic called her Val, she was reminded of the day they met. The day when a bunch of the neighborhood kids were going to the movies and Val had been forced to sit in Dominic's lap in the backseat of his brother's car. The ride was only five minutes, but it changed Valentina's life. She was just fifteen.

"It'll be just like the old times," Valentina said, and smiled.

Fifty-Five

Ursella looked around at the house. Her home, where she'd raised her only child. She took such pride in it. How foolish she had been.

She started in the entryway. That was where the broker would begin his tour. The Italian marble flooring, after all these years, still looked impeccable. It hadn't scuffed, it hadn't lost its shine. And the pattern was very much still in style.

The edges of Ursella's mouth turned up as she moved to the dining room. The millwork was impeccable. Would this broker realize that? When she'd decided to paint the entire room a deep navy, mouldings included, she'd been right. Even though her decorator advised her against it, she knew that it would create an intimate atmosphere, perfect for dinner parties that lasted long into the night. Flanked by floor-to-ceiling windows, the dark walls created the perfect contrast to the flood of light the room got. And navy was the perfect backdrop for one of her most prized possessions—the Kandinsky that Edmond had bought for her at auction on their first anniversary.

Ursella sat down in the living room. Edmond's father's secretary desk sat in one corner, an antique card table in the other.

She took her shoes off and rubbed her toes on the hand-knotted Oriental rug. Then she put her feet onto the leather ottoman. This room was perfect—nothing more had to be done. She could sit and wait.

The broker would be coming at eleven. "Just to take a look," he had said. "To show you how to stage it for the market." As if Ursella needed to be told. More foolishness.

After she had married Edmond, Ursella had learned everything she could about design. She studied the homes of his friends, of his family, to learn how they lived. She wanted a home that looked just like theirs. Just as refined. Just as beautiful. Just as rich. And, of course, she hired the most expensive interior designer she could find. The one Edmond's mother had used, the one all his friends used.

Her home was immaculate. Perfect. Above reproach.

Yet someone was about to come tell her all the things that were wrong with it. All the ways the house wouldn't be worth what Ursella thought it was worth. Ursella and Edmond had decided on an asking price. But the house was worth so much more than any number. Every room, every square inch of it held a precious memory. Ursella didn't know how she would let it go.

The broker was a squirrely man. Ursella detested him immediately. He arranged his thin hair like a nest on top of his head, and he had an equally thin mustache to match. Ursella thought that men who wore thin mustaches were unmanly. When he shook Ursella's hand, he pursed his lips, as if she were his dinner and he was ready to eat. His suit was ill-fitting, and his pants were hemmed too high. He spoke very fast, and asked her if she could understand what he was saying, what with English being her second language and all. He then tried to guess at her accent. Ursella found the whole exchange distasteful. And tacky. If there was one thing Ursella didn't like, it was tacky.

She gave him a tour of the house, and he oohed and aahed at all the appropriate intervals. He loved the mouldings, original to the town house, and the wood inlays in her floor, also original. He praised her choice of lighting, her window treatments, and fabric choices for the furniture. The broker especially loved the Chagall that hung in her bedroom, a wedding gift from her husband, bought on their honeymoon in the South of France.

Ursella relaxed. Everything would be all right.

"Why don't we go to the kitchen for a cup of tea?" she asked. Maybe she had rushed to judgment? After all, he couldn't help it if his legs were too skinny, if his eyes were too beady, if his hair was too thin.

Ursella poured water into a kettle—she hated using the instant hot water faucet they had at the sink, a kettle was the only way to prepare a proper cup of tea—and selected her favorite box of English teas from Harrods. She only offered these teas on special occasions. She hoped he could see that.

"Let's talk price," the broker said, before Ursella had even had a chance to sit down. Before she was even able to pour the tea.

When he called out a number that was 30 percent less than what Ursella and Edmond had decided on, Ursella dropped the teacup she had been holding. It fell onto the floor as if in slow motion. One minute, Ursella saw it in her hand, and the next it was falling, slowly, gracefully, onto her Italian porcelain tile floor. It crashed down and broke into a million pieces. Ursella was too shocked to even make a move to clean it up. She simply stared at it, at the tiny little pieces, as the broker continued speaking.

The market has changed.

There's not a lot of interest in these big properties right now, at least not at that price point.

The tastes of the house are too specific to you and your family. Would you agree to have it professionally staged? Repaint the dining room?

Ursella didn't know what she wanted to do anymore. She certainly didn't want to sell her home for less than it was worth. And now she was questioning the plan she and Edmond had come up with—to sell the Manhattan town house and camp out at their summer home in Nice. Suddenly, Ursella didn't want to go to France. She didn't want to leave the city. She didn't ever want to leave her house.

"I'll be in touch," she said, once she regained her composure. "Thank you for your time."

She sat down at the kitchen table with a fresh cup of tea and had her housekeeper show the unctuous little man to the door.

Fifty-Six

"Have you spoken to Gid?" Becca asked Sarah.

Henry had taken a train out to the beach ("I needed to get some studying done on the way out," he'd explained), and was now firing up the grill. He had insisted on manning the barbecue.

"Has he ever cooked anything before in his life?" Joe whispered to Sarah.

He had not. But that didn't dull his enthusiasm. After all, how hard could it be to cook up some hamburgers and hot dogs?

"We had a video chat," Sarah said.

"How come Gid never tries to video chat with me?" Becca asked.

"How come *you* never try to video chat with *him*?" Sarah asked back.

Becca ignored the question. "Mom said he's re-upped with the program. And that Malika dumped him and left."

"You spoke to Mom?" Sarah asked. She tried to sound casual, but everyone knew it was a loaded question.

"Yeah, haven't you?" Becca tried for her own casual tone. She was far more convincing. The beach had done something to her. Everything about her seemed calmer. Quieter. More relaxed, more fun.

"Barely," Sarah said. "She's still mad about—"

"She's mad at me, too," Becca said. "But I guess she can only freeze out one daughter at a time."

The girls both laughed.

"How's school?" Joe asked. He really wanted to ask why Henry hadn't seasoned the hamburger meat. He made a mental note to add salt and pepper to his burger. And barbecue sauce and ketchup. And pickles.

"Great, man," Henry said. "I've been asked to be a teaching assistant in my sociology class and I am stoked."

"Cool," Joe said. "What does a teaching assistant do?"

"I have no idea," Henry said, laughing. "But I'm excited to figure it out."

"You were asked to be a teaching assistant after only one semester?" Sarah asked from across the backyard.

"Isn't that impressive?" Becca said.

"It's something," Sarah said.

Henry tried to flip the burgers, but they broke apart on the spatula. No one had told him that you needed to sear the first side so that the burger wouldn't fall apart when you tried to flip it. Joe didn't think he should be the person to point that out. "It's really great."

"Happy to hear it," Joe said.

"Is this the same Henry I met at Passover?" Sarah whispered to her sister. Becca just shrugged her shoulders.

"I'm a good influence on everyone but myself," Becca finally said.

Sarah ignored the self-pity. "Do you think you're going back in the fall?" she asked.

"I'm not even going to think about it until August," Becca said. "I'm letting go. I'm not going to think about anything."

Sarah could tell by her sister's appearance just how much she had "let go." She wouldn't mention her sister's hair, badly in need of a cut, or her legs, badly in need of a shave. She thought about suggesting manicures and pedicures, her treat, but she held herself back. That would be the sort of thing Sylvia would say. Still, Becca caught her staring at her sand-encrusted feet.

"What?" she said.

"Nothing," Sarah replied.

"I just came off the beach!" Becca said. "Of course my feet are sandy!"

Sarah had just come off the beach, too. But she had taken the time to have a shower before dinner.

Joe could see the wheels in Sarah's head turning. He couldn't have her feuding with yet another family member. And more importantly, it was only Tuesday. He couldn't take a week of arguing. It was enough that Sarah was on edge because of her mother.

"Did you know that the Last Supper was actually a Passover Seder?" he asked.

Everyone stopped for a moment. It was so out of the blue, so apropos of nothing, that no one knew what to say for a second.

"No," Sarah said. "I did not know that. How do *you* know that?"

"Rabbi Weisman told me," he said.

"Who?" Henry said. He abandoned his post at the grill to listen to what was unfolding.

"Since when do you pal around with my mother's rabbi?" Sarah asked. It came out sounding like an accusation, but she'd meant for it to come out sounding jovial. Flirty, even.

"I'm taking a class with him," Joe said, as if nice Italian boys took classes with Jewish rabbis all the time.

"What sort of class?" Sarah asked.

"We can talk about it later," Joe said.

"We can talk about it now," Sarah said. She was no longer going for jovial. Or flirty. She wanted to know what Joe was talking about.

"It's a class on Judaism," Joe said.

"Dude, are you converting?" Henry asked.

"I'm thinking about it," Joe said. He shrugged his shoulders and took a sip of his beer.

"Why wouldn't you tell me that?" Sarah asked.

"I wasn't sure it would stick," Joe said.

"So, why are you telling me now?"

"I think it's stuck."

Becca jumped from her seat and ran to Joe. She hugged him tightly, sand coming loose from every part of her body. It sprinkled into his hair, onto his shirt, and all over his jeans. "*Mazel tov!*" she yelled into his ear. She hadn't meant to yell directly into his ear, but she was excited and got a bit carried away.

"You're all sandy!" Sarah said. "Stop hugging him!"

"A little sand never killed anyone," Becca said. "In fact, a little dirt and mess is okay, isn't it? I'm learning to embrace the dirt."

"That's what you've learned since you've been out here?" Sarah asked. "That you skipped your internship for? Are you about to leave for a cabin in the woods, never to be seen again?"

"No." Becca laughed. "I'm just learning to embrace whatever comes. To let things go. Maybe you'll learn that, too."

"Learn what?" Sarah said.

"You have to let go."

Sarah took a sip of her wine and studied her sister.

"Let go of what, exactly?" Sarah asked.

The answer Becca would have provided, if given the opportunity, was this: *Something. Everything. Anything that's not important. The things that drive you crazy. The things that make you tear the hairs out of your head, one by one. The idea that we have to be perfect, the idea that we have to be good, the idea that we can be happy when all we're trying to do is live up to someone else's expectations. I felt it, I know you feel it, too—the weight of what we're expected to do. What people want us to be. Let go of all of it and just be. See where that takes you. Yes, your feet will be caked in sand, and you'll be in desperate need of a shower, but you might just like it.*

But Becca didn't get to say any of that. In fact, she didn't get a chance to say anything at all. The hamburgers caught fire, and in an instant, the entire grill was lit up with bright red flames. Becca grabbed a pitcher of water and tried to douse the fire. The flames leapt higher into the air, threatening to light the fence behind the grill and the deck it stood on.

"Get back," Henry said, shielding the girls with his arms and trying to get them to back away from the fire.

"Is there an extinguisher in the house?" Joe asked. Becca didn't know, so she yelled for help instead.

The firefighters would later tell her that it was a grease fire and that it wasn't actually Henry's fault. In fact, there was nothing he could have done to prevent it. The grill had never been cleaned properly, so it was just a matter of time before this grill joined the July parade of grill fires. The firemen told them that pouring water onto the grill was the very thing that made the fire blaze out of control. You never add water to a grease fire. You must snuff it out by depriving it of oxygen. A lid large enough to cover it would have done the trick, or even a simple box of baking soda.

Andy came running out of the house, completely naked, holding an extinguisher. He pulled the pin, squeezed the handle, and doused the flames. It took a few tries, but he got the fire out. A minute later, the skinny girlfriend came out in a towel, and handed one to him. They walked back into the house without saying a word.

Becca went to Kmart and bought five boxes of baking soda the next day.

Fifty-Seven

Sylvia loved summer weddings. Especially when the weather cooperated. She loved the twilight most of all—the ceremony unfolding as the sun dipped below the trees, the champagne and hors d'oeuvres being served as light gave way to dusk, and finally, dancing with her darling Alan as the moon and the stars revealed themselves. How lovely to celebrate a wedding at that magical time of day.

Sylvia tried not to let it bother her that her friend Muriel's daughter was marrying a nice Jewish doctor. The girl was the same age as Sarah, and already she had secured a high-powered job as an attorney at a top Manhattan firm. The groom had graduated Albert Einstein College of Medicine and was about to embark on a fellowship in neurology. He was handsome, too.

"The bride could have lost a little weight before the wedding," she whispered over canapés and peach martinis. "Don't you think?"

"That's a terrible thing to say," Alan chastised. "The bride is beautiful. All brides are beautiful."

Sylvia stuffed a bite of wild salmon on a cucumber into her mouth.

"I always wanted to throw a summer wedding," she said, looking out at the golf course. The greens were looking lovely. "I thought it would be so pretty to set up a tent in our backyard."

"You could still do that," Alan said, taking Sylvia's hand. When she looked off in the distance like that, with that wistful expression on her face, Alan was reminded of when they first met, when they first started dating. He never could tell what Sylvia was thinking in those days. And now?

"I don't think Becca and Henry will last the year," Sylvia said, taking a measured sip of her cocktail. "And Malika left Gideon."

"You have another daughter."

"She's already married," Sylvia said, turning to face Alan. "Secretly married, don't you know? It's all anyone around here can talk about."

"I think you're exaggerating."

"So I'm exaggerating. But still—why would I need to throw her a wedding?"

"An olive branch?"

"An olive branch!" Sylvia cried. "She should feel lucky that I haven't disowned her. I'm not extending any sort of olive branch. *She* should extend an olive branch to *me*."

"I think she wants to," Alan said quietly, "but you won't speak to her."

"I've spoken to her."

"Why don't you talk to her?" Alan asked. "I mean really talk to her?"

"She hasn't called."

"Yes, she has."

"Well," Sylvia reasoned. "She hasn't said the right thing."

"What do you want her to say?" Alan asked. "I'm sure if you told her, she'd say it." Alan was upset with Sarah, too. Furious, in fact. He understood why Sarah hadn't told Sylvia, but why hadn't she told him? They had a good relationship, didn't they? How could she tell Valentina and Dominic, but not him? It consumed his thoughts, this cataloging of old memories, trying to figure out where things had changed. When he had lost Sarah.

But Sylvia's anger took over everything; it swallowed everything whole. There was simply no room for Alan to be angry. No time for it. All he could do was duck and cover, hope that he didn't get Sylvia angry and start another fight. A bigger fight. A fight that couldn't be undone.

He wanted Sarah to apologize. Of course he did. But he had to prioritize. Sylvia needed to be okay with things first. It was all about Sarah and Sylvia. It always was.

"How do we move past this?" Alan asked.

"I don't know," Sylvia shouted. "I have no idea."

Alan was aware that other wedding guests had turned to stare at them, but he didn't care. He asked Sylvia: "How can she make things right again?"

"I don't know."

"Why don't we start by accepting one of her invitations?" Alan offered. "Why don't we see what she has to say?"

"I'm still too angry," Sylvia said.

"Okay, sweetheart," Alan said. "Okay."

The father-daughter dance was usually Alan's favorite part of the wedding. He loved being part of such a momentous occasion in the lives of his friends and family. But not tonight. He looked over at Sylvia, and saw that her lips were smiling, but her eyes were not. She took a generous sip of her drink, and Alan followed her lead.

Midway through the song, the bandleader invited Muriel and her new son-in-law to the dance floor. The kids had taken dance lessons, that much Alan could tell. Muriel's son-in-law took Muriel's hand, and they danced the waltz. Muriel beamed with pride, smiling widely as they moved. Alan looked at her son-in-law and saw him counting out the steps: 1-2-3, 1-2-3.

Alan reached for Sylvia's hand and she gave it to him. She squeezed his hand tightly, and Alan rubbed hers with his thumb. They sat like that for the rest of the dance, holding hands, watching but not really watching, waiting for the song to end.

Fifty-Eight

The government came to investigate Edmond's bank. He didn't really understand why they were there. The bank had failed. Didn't businesses fail all the time? But the Feds wanted to make sure there was no criminal activity involved. There wasn't.

Was there?

Forensic accountants had taken over the bank's accounting department; federal agents were in every office. Even Edmond's personal computer had been seized. Edmond knew they wouldn't find any illegal activity. (Would they?) Just bad decision after bad decision. With more bad decisions made to try to make up for the first ones. (What was that expression—throwing good money after bad?) But what Edmond didn't know was how long it would take the government to figure this out. Or how badly the Feds wanted to make an example of him.

So, on Thursday, instead of subjecting himself to another day of sideways stares and looks of disappointment, anger, and pity, Edmond played hooky. He took the town car to Midtown, like he did every day. He even made it as far as the elevator banks. But he couldn't bring himself to go in. He couldn't bring himself to push the button to the fourteenth floor, to open the door to the same office he'd gone to, day after day, since he was twenty years old. He stood in the elevator bank, surrounded by young executives pounding away on their smart phones, and had the inescapable feeling that he simply didn't belong there. He used to be like these other people—driven, single-minded in his quest to make money (more money than the next guy), and be successful (more successful than the next guy). But why? Where had it gotten him? His wife was barely speaking to him. His family home was on the market. And as far as he could tell, his only son was lost to him.

He had a sudden desire to visit Central Park. He'd lived in Manhattan for most of his life, but he could count the times he'd been in the park as an adult on one hand. How could that be? He walked in at Fifty-Ninth and Fifth.

Edmond had memories of visiting the park as a child. The nanny—always the nanny—would take Edmond and his brothers into the park to play. Their favorite spot was Bethesda Fountain. They would bring a ball and play in circles while their nanny watched them from her perch on the edge of the fountain. They weren't allowed to climb the steps without her, and they weren't allowed to get too close to The Lake. Even in wintertime, she would bundle them up in wool sweaters, heavy coats, and boots so that they could play in the fresh air. His nanny was always talking about "getting the children fresh air." He'd forgotten about that until he found himself at the fountain.

It was different from how he remembered it. The fountain was the same, the beautiful angel perched high on top, but somehow the space felt different. Edmond and his brothers had always thought of this as their secret place—the lower passage their secret walkway to a hidden spot. Now, the terrace was filled with tourists, mothers with baby strollers, and street musicians. The space was filled with artists drawing, sketching, and painting, with vendors selling popcorn, hot dogs, and pretzels. Edmond stopped to buy a pretzel and a soda.

He sat down on the edge of the fountain and took a bite of his pretzel. Salty, crisp on the outside, and soft on the inside. It tasted like New York. He tore open one of those little packets of mustard to squirt onto the pretzel, and a few spots landed right on his light-pink Hermès tie. He started to get angry—at himself, at the stupid vendor who'd insisted that he use mustard—but really, what did it matter? He had no meetings to attend, no office to go to, and no reason to be all dressed up in the middle of a gorgeous summer day. He took his tie off and carefully folded it before placing it in the inside pocket of his suit jacket.

Next off, his jacket. The sun was beaming down, hot and strong, and he rolled up the sleeves of his dress shirt as well. He could practically hear Ursella chiding him about using sunscreen, but surely a little sun never hurt anyone? When did the sun become our enemy anyway? Hadn't he recently read an article in *The Wall Street Journal* about how important vitamin D was and how schoolchildren, constantly slathered in sunscreen, were beginning to exhibit severe vitamin D deficiencies?

He took a sip of his soft drink. Without any ice to break down the gases, thousands of tiny bubbles tickled his throat. He couldn't remember the last time he'd had soda. He couldn't remember the last time he'd bought food from a vendor. If pressed to really think about it, he was certain he'd never been in Central Park as an adult in the middle of the week.

Then Edmond did something rather uncharacteristic. He took off his shoes. He sat, in the middle of Central Park, in the middle of a workday, with no shoes on. Eating a pretzel. With mustard. He closed his eyes for a moment and tilted his head back. He could feel the warm rays of the sun on his face.

The Feds were in his office, reading every paper, every e-mail, every text message. Their accountants were poring over every number, every figure, every formula his bank had ever calculated. He'd been interviewed, interrogated, and examined. And here he sat, in the center of Central Park, barefoot.

It seemed kind of perfect.

Fifty-Nine

"Hello," Sylvia said. She had a tone. There was definitely a tone.

"Hiya, Mrs. Gold," Joe said, and walked over to give her a kiss hello.

"Hello, Sylvia," Rabbi Weisman said, before rushing over to give her one of those warm hugs he was famous for.

She turned to Joe. "What are you doing here?"

She knew what she was doing—paying the yearly membership fees, getting her seat assignment for the High Holiday services. She could not, for the life of her, figure out what Joe would be doing at her synagogue. And in Rabbi Weisman's office, no less. Did the rabbi own an expensive foreign car? Was the rabbi having car trouble? Was this a house call?

"He's one of my most promising students," Rabbi Weisman said. "But class is about to begin, so we must go."

"Class?" Sylvia asked.

Sure, Rabbi Weisman's class was about to begin, but a temple member was still a temple member, and if said temple member wanted some of the rabbi's time, he would not say no.

"It's our Introduction to Judaism class," the rabbi said. "It's a wonderful—"

Sylvia wasn't really interested in how wonderful the class was. To Joe, she said: "Are you converting?"

"That's certainly an option at the end of class," the rabbi answered for him. "But that's a decision Joe can make any time he wants."

"So, no," Sylvia said.

"Not yet," Joe clarified.

Sylvia looked at Joe. He smiled at her, a mouthful of perfectly white teeth. She did not smile back at him.

"It was lovely to see you today, Sylvia," the rabbi said, and motioned Joe into his office.

"You, too, Rabbi Weisman," Sylvia said as she made her way into the bookkeeper's office.

"That Sylvia keeps you on your toes, I bet," Rabbi Weisman said to Joe.

"That's one way to put it," Joe said. He sat down in a chair across from the rabbi. He set his textbook and notebook onto the rabbi's desk.

"Does she want you to convert?" Rabbi Weisman asked.

"She wants me to not be married to her daughter," Joe said.

Rabbi Weisman regarded him. "Do you think, perhaps, she's angry about the way she found out?"

"I think she's angry about everything," Joe said. "She doesn't think I'm good enough for Sarah; she doesn't want us together, much less married."

"But you *are* married now."

"Yes," Joe said.

"So, she'll have to learn to deal with it."

"I suppose," Joe said. "Or she can keep avoiding Sarah. They've barely spoken in months."

"Do you think Sylvia would approve of your relationship if you converted to Judaism?"

"I'd still be a garage rat," Joe said. "So, no."

"Don't call yourself that," Rabbi Weisman said. "You're a small business owner. And a valuable contributor to our local community and economy."

"That's how Sylvia sees me," Joe said. "A garage rat. A piece of garbage. Unworthy of her fancy daughter. But it doesn't really matter. I'm not doing this for Sylvia. I'm doing it for Sarah."

"You should do it for yourself," Rabbi Weisman said. "Now, shall we begin?"

Sixty

"Do you think we should include the Rothschilds in our New Year plans?" Sylvia asked.

"You're thinking of New Year's Eve? It's only August!" Alan said. "How very motivated of you."

"I mean Jewish New Year," Sylvia corrected, though she could tell from Alan's tone that he already knew that. "Rosh Hashanah."

"If Becca wants the Rothschilds to be there," Alan said. "That would be lovely."

What he didn't say, but Sylvia knew he was thinking was: *if Becca plans to still be seeing Henry come September.*

"I'll check with Becca, then."

"Who else are we planning on having?" Alan asked. With Gideon still in Sri Lanka, he knew that Sylvia would know what he was asking. Would Sarah be there?

"Sarah seemed to think that she and Joe could make it," she informed Alan. "But she'd have to check with Valentina and Dominic."

Alan wanted to play it cool, really he did. If he'd had a moment to think about it, he would have said something casual, like: *Well, that's nice, honey. Let me know what happens.* But he didn't have a moment to think about it. And he couldn't contain himself. "You invited Valentina and Dominic?"

"Yes," Sylvia said. She said it calmly, daring Alan to press on. "They *are* family now, aren't they?"

"I suppose they are," he said.

"I may not be speaking to Sarah at the present moment," Sylvia said, "but a holiday is still a holiday."

Sixty-One

"I found these at that shop around the corner from my house . . . I thought you'd like them for the holiday," Sarah said.

She handed Sylvia the gift—the peace offering—and Sylvia handled it as if it might be flammable.

"What is it?" she asked, turning the small package over in her hands, as if the simple act of holding it, turning it, would reveal to her its contents.

"Open it!" Sarah said. She hoped her mother would love her present. It was a set of linen cocktail napkins, embroidered with tiny apples. The perfect thing to use for the start of her Rosh Hashanah dinner when apples and honey would be passed around to celebrate the coming of a sweet new year.

"Maybe later," Sylvia said. "I'm so busy. You should have called before you came over."

Sarah's face fell. She had thought that the invitation to Rosh Hashanah was Sylvia's way of offering forgiveness. She could see now—and only now—that she had been sorely mistaken.

"You're still mad," Sarah said.

Sylvia regarded her daughter for a moment. Sarah stood before her, as if ready for judgment. Sylvia laughed out loud.

"I'm sorry," Sarah said. "I don't know how many times I can say it. I'm sorry. I'm sorry, I'm sorry, I'm sorry! What else can I say? What else can I do?"

"You think it's that easy?"

"No," Sarah said. "I don't! I just need you to forgive me, and I don't know how to get you to do that. I'm sorry. Don't you understand? I'm so sorry."

"How dare you," Sylvia snarled. "How dare you do that to me? How dare you rob me of that experience?"

"I'm sorry," Sarah said. Again. It seemed like she couldn't say she was sorry quite enough. "I knew you wouldn't have approved. I know you don't like Joe, don't think he's good enough for me. I did it for me. For us."

"You don't even realize that you took something from me," Sylvia said. "From your father. Who do you think you are?"

Sylvia was yelling. Sarah didn't know how to react. Her mother didn't yell. Sylvia generally spoke quietly, softly. If you really wanted to hear her, you had to pay attention. You had to get close. Sarah wasn't sure if she'd ever heard her mother yell before. Tears streamed down her face before she realized she was crying.

"Why are *you* crying?" Sylvia said. "*I* should be the one crying. *I* was the one made to be a fool, made to be a laughingstock in my own home, at my own family holiday dinner."

"I didn't mean to do that," Sarah said. "I was just afraid."

"Afraid of *what*, exactly?"

"Of you."

Sixty-Two

"She is such a spoiled brat," Sylvia ranted.

"So spoiled," Alan parroted back.

"How did we raise such spoiled children?" Sylvia asked. "I'm so angry."

"So angry," Alan said.

"And she has the nerve to cry?"

"The nerve," Alan said.

"I should have really let her have it," Sylvia said.

"It sounds like you did," Alan said.

"Excuse me?" Sylvia put down her knife and fork. She stared across the table at Alan, who was still cutting a piece of broccoli. He speared a tiny floret and put it into his mouth. Sylvia continued to stare. Alan looked up and saw her watching him, waiting. For what? He wasn't entirely sure.

"I'm only saying that it sounds like you were able to get a few things off your chest today," Alan said, clearing his throat. "I wish I'd had the opportunity to do the same."

"Yes," Sylvia said, regaining her composure. "Well."

"Are we going to let this be the end?"

"The end of what?"

"The end of our relationship with our daughter," Alan said. "What she did was bad. Inexcusable, really. I don't know if I'll ever be able to forgive her. I know I won't forget it. But are we going to let it break our family apart?"

"I haven't done anything here," Sylvia said. "I am the injured party."

"You are. We are," Alan corrected.

"Okay, then."

"But we're also the parents," Alan said. "You're going to have to decide when it's time to let this go and move on. Do you think you can do that?"

"Yes," Sylvia said.

"Great," Alan said. "Do you know when that will be?"

"No."

Sixty-Three

"That can't be," Sylvia said. "That just can't be."

"I'm afraid so, Mrs. Gold," the landscaper said. "If you look right here, it's attaching to the house."

Sylvia was out in her front yard with her landscaper, Charlie. He had left a note under her front door the day before, stating he had something URGENT to discuss with her. She couldn't imagine what that could be—a hydrangea emergency?— but met with him just to be certain.

"I saw that," Sylvia said. She gently touched the ivy that was climbing the bricks of her house. "I thought it looked beautiful. Makes the house look more distinguished."

"That may be," he said, "but it's going to tear your whole house down."

"That's a bit dramatic, don't you think?" Sylvia said, laughter in her voice.

"No," Charlie said. "It's not. Crumbling mortar or small cracks can be invaded by the ivy roots. You have a broken brick right here, for example."

Sylvia's eye went to the broken brick. Why hadn't she noticed that before? Were there others like it? "What's your suggestion?"

"I say we take it down before it gets out of control," Charlie said. "Right now, it's manageable. It won't be too difficult to contain the damage. But if we let it go any further, I can't make any guarantees."

"But I've worked so hard on it," Sylvia said. "Do you have any idea how much effort I've put into this?"

"I'm sorry, Mrs. Gold, but I don't see any other way. You've done a great job training the ivy, really you have. But is it worth destroying your house over?"

"It's not going to destroy my house. What an overstatement," Sylvia said, furrowing her brow. As if anyone or anything could tear down the house that she and Alan had built. What they'd created together. What they shared.

"And anyway, here down by the base of your house, this is some perfect cover for rats and mice and other unsavory creatures," he said.

"I do not have rats and mice," Sylvia said, her tone clipped.

"Yet."

"Now you're just trying to scare me," Sylvia said. He was overstepping. A warning was one thing, but what this man was suggesting was patently ridiculous. Perhaps *he* was the unsavory creature she should be keeping away from her house.

"I've seen it before," Charlie said. "You want to nip these problems in the bud. See here?" He pulled a bit of the root away from Sylvia's brick house. "The roots leave this glue-like substance. The only way to get it off is with old-fashioned elbow grease."

Sylvia looked at where the ivy had been removed. She picked at the hairy tendrils with her fingernail. It had no give to it. It would take a hard scrub brush to get rid of the mess. Hours of work.

"So, do you want me to get started on the removal?" he asked. "I could have my crew out here tomorrow."

"I suppose so," Sylvia said, taking a vine and winding it around her hand. She gently tugged and the entire thing dislodged itself from the house.

"Okay, we'll get started first thing," Charlie said. "Like I said, I really am sorry to be the bearer of bad news. You did a really great job with the vines."

"Thank you," Sylvia said, grabbing another ivy vine, not looking at Charlie.

"You have a tiny bit of poison ivy on the edge over there," he said, pointing at the corner of the house. "I wouldn't do that without gloves."

Sixty-Four

"Jesus Christ, Sarah, I thought you'd be happy for me."

"I *am* happy," Sarah said. "But now Mom *really* isn't going to ever forgive me."

"Because, yeah," Becca said. "My decision to go back to medical school is really all about *you*."

Becca hung up the phone before Sarah could get a word in. Sarah really hated when Becca did that. Sarah supposed it had something to do with being the baby of the family. Becca had never really outgrown the baby role, even in her adult life.

And it was so like Becca to do something like that—to turn something normal, something average, into a grand announcement. To actually make telephone calls to announce to your friends and family that your summer sabbatical is over, and that you've decided to return to medical school come fall. As if your friends and family didn't already know that that's what you'd be doing. Becca may have taken the summer off, but she was who she was, and there was no changing that.

Perhaps she was trying to distract from the scandal enveloping the Rothschild clan. It looked like the Boyfriend's father was to be indicted any day now, so maybe Becca was trying to soften the blow of jail time for her possible future father-in-law by announcing that she, herself, was back on the straight and narrow.

Sarah couldn't help but chuckle at the turn of events. Her mother had been so excited, so nervous, about welcoming the Rothschilds into her family, and now Edmond would be going to jail. Just like Dominic.

Well, not just like Dominic. Rich people didn't go to jail the way regular people went to jail. But Sarah liked this new turn of events all the same.

Sixty-Five

Valentina knew she shouldn't have listened to Dominic. "Wear what you like," he had said. "You always look great," he had said. "If there's one thing I know about my Val it's that she always dresses right for the occasion." But she was dressed all wrong. What was she thinking wearing a snug-fitting knit dress? Everyone here favored white blouses and skirts. All of the women wore hose or tights; no one was bare-legged like she was. And hats. So many of the women were wearing hats! Dressed for the occasion indeed. She looked like she was going out to a sexy dinner in Manhattan, not religious services.

But none of that mattered when she saw her Joey sitting in the front row near the rabbi. She knew that he was getting some sort of honor today where he'd get to read from the Torah. She couldn't wait for his big moment.

Valentina wasn't altogether pleased about his possible conversion, but here, in a house of worship, she allowed herself to wonder what God had really done for her, anyway. God had given Sylvia three healthy kids, so maybe he'd do the same for her Joey. It was the Jewish New Year, so like every New Year's

Eve, she thought about the year to come. Maybe Sarah would get pregnant. Maybe they'd make her a grandmother.

"Are they going to be speaking in Hebrew the whole time?" Dominic whispered. Only Dominic's whisper was gruff. And loud.

"Shh!" she chided. Wasn't it enough that they stood out from the crowd? Did Dominic have to draw even more attention to them by talking? She gave Sylvia a look that said: *I can't believe he's speaking!* Sylvia smiled back at her warmly. Even when they weren't in her home, she was a gracious hostess. Now that was class.

"The rabbi's sermon will be in English," Edmond said to Dominic.

Edmond looked every bit the titan of industry in a perfectly tailored charcoal-gray suit and cherry-red tie. Valentina wished she'd insisted on Dominic wearing a suit. He'd come in dress pants and a shirt. No jacket. No tie. The outline of his sleeveless undershirt was visible through his shirt.

Joe walked up to the bimah for his big honor. Valentina sat up a little straighter in her seat. She was so pleased when Sarah told her that Joe would be getting this honor, this *aliyah*. Dominic, less so.

Dominic didn't understand what else Joe needed to do for these people. Joe and Sarah were married, for Christ's sake. Why did Joe have something else to prove? When would it end? When would it ever be enough? Valentina tried to explain that Joe just wanted to be closer to Sarah. To cement their bond. To be able to make an informed decision about how to raise their future children. Dominic softened at the mention of children. Valentina always knew exactly what to say to her Dominic.

Sarah stood at Joe's side as he read directly from the Torah, her hat tilted at just the right angle. Joe's Hebrew was amazing, Valentina thought, even though she didn't know what it should sound like. But from the expression on Sarah's face, she could tell he was doing well.

When Sarah had explained what the services would be like (maybe she'd told her to wear a white blouse and a skirt ... but there'd been no mention of a hat), she said that Joe would be conducting part of the service with the rabbi. This sounded very exciting to Valentina; her priest had never asked her to take part in a service before. Sarah was very clear about the rules: there would be no applause after Joe read. He was just reading a part of the service, and once he was done with his *aliyah*, he would come back and sit with the congregation. The service would continue as it had before. Yes, it was an honor, the highest you could get during the High Holiday season. But no, there would not be applause.

Valentina relayed this information to Dominic, but he wasn't interested. He wasn't really interested in anything having to do with this Jewish holiday. He didn't want to go back to Sylvia's after temple to eat, much less to listen to his son speak in a language he couldn't understand.

Joe finished reading, and the rabbi shook his hand. Sarah smiled widely and kissed Joe on the cheek. Valentina felt herself brimming with pride. She just couldn't help herself. She had planned to wait until Joe got back to his seat, and then give him a warm hug and congratulate him for doing so well. Just like Sylvia would have done. But Valentina was so overcome with emotion, so overcome with pride, that she forgot all about her plan and jumped from her seat, clapping wildly.

"Great job, Joey!" she cried, then mouthed, *Sorry!* as soon as she remembered the no-applause rule.

Edmond said: "That *was* rather good!" and Ursella reached out to pat her back. Valentina didn't dare look at Sylvia for a reaction.

"That *was* very good," the rabbi agreed from up at his podium. "That was Joseph Russo, one of my Introduction to Judaism students. He's just learning Hebrew now. Wasn't that wonderful?"

And with that, the congregation fell into thunderous applause. From the corner of her eye, Valentina could almost make out Sylvia, standing up from her chair, clapping.

Sixty-Six

"I've been thinking a lot lately about forgiveness," Rabbi Weisman began.

Alan put his arm around the back of Sylvia's chair and settled in to listen. It seemed to Sylvia that he wanted her to pay close attention to what she was about to hear.

"The days between Rosh Hashanah, the Jewish New Year, and Yom Kippur, the Day of Atonement, are called the Days of Awe," he continued. "And why are they called that? The dictionary defines awe as: 'an emotion variously combining dread, veneration, and wonder that is inspired by authority or by the sacred or sublime.'" Rabbi Weisman was big on dictionary definitions. And not just any dictionary—*Merriam Webster's Collegiate Dictionary*. Eleventh edition.

"It is during the Days of Awe that God opens the Book of Life, to see what is written. On Yom Kippur, we pray for forgiveness for our sins. God makes his final determination and then closes the Book of Life. It remains sealed until the following year.

"But before one can ask God for forgiveness on Yom Kippur, before one can be written in the Book of Life for another year, one must first consider the relationships we have. With friends. With family." The rabbi took a long pause before continuing. "The High Holy season is a time to reflect. To think. To forgive. To ask for forgiveness."

Sylvia looked over at her children. First, at Becca, seated next to Ursella with Henry on her other side, fingers entwined. And then to Sarah. Joe had his arm draped lazily over the back of her chair, much in the same way that Alan had his over her own chair. Sarah's head tilted slightly toward Joe. She was paying attention to her husband, letting him know she was beside him, even as they listened intently to the rabbi's words. Her husband.

And now, here was Joe, learning about Judaism. Not for her, but for Sarah. Wasn't that something?

"At this time of year, I'm always reminded of the story of Jacob and Esau. Younger brother Jacob, who stole his brother's birthright and his blessing, was exiled from his homeland. When God told him to return twenty years later, Jacob realized that he would have to pass through his brother Esau's territory. Jacob was scared. He knew that his brother wanted to kill him for all that he had done. Jacob did what he could to prepare—he sent presents, he sent men to spy. Esau, also readying himself for the meeting, surrounded himself with an army of four hundred men.

"When the moment arrived for the brothers to reunite, Jacob did not know what to expect. Would his brother kill him? When Esau saw Jacob, he didn't kill him. He embraced him. He kissed him. He forgave him.

"It reminds me of two congregants I had when I was back in New York. Two brothers. Business partners. When their father died, the younger brother—let's call him Jacob—asked his older brother to use the entire inheritance to start a company. The thing they'd dreamed of since they were young. They invested the money, all the money they had in the world, and the company was a failure. The older brother, let's call him Esau, lost everything. He had to sell his house and move in with his in-laws. The younger brother, Jacob, was shunned by the family and went off to California. In California, he created another company, a better company, and he became a huge success.

"His older brother never forgave him. 'Why was the second company the one that succeeded?' he asked me. 'Doesn't my brother owe me something?'

"They didn't speak for twenty years. Jacob didn't come back East for holidays, he didn't attend the Bar Mitzvahs of his nephews. And then the fight was no longer about the money. It became about other things, like the fact that Jacob never called on the holidays to wish his brother a *gut yontiff*, and the fact that he'd missed so many milestones. He'd missed so many chances to say 'I'm sorry' that it became impossible to do so. There were just too many apologies to be made, too many things to be angry about.

"When their mother got sick, her dying wish was for Jacob to come and see her.

"So, Jacob flew back to New York for the first time in twenty years. It seemed like Esau had an army of four hundred men— the entire family hadn't spoken to Jacob in the twenty years he'd been gone, and Esau had many close friends, friends who felt like family to him, ready to do battle for him.

"He saw his brother and was prepared to fight. But when Esau saw his little brother, the money didn't matter anymore. What mattered was that his brother was home. They were family.

"Forgiveness."

Alan passed Sylvia a handkerchief before she'd even realized that she was tearing up. Under normal circumstances, she'd excuse herself to use the ladies' room. But no one ever got up in the middle of one of Rabbi Weisman's sermons. She dabbed the handkerchief to the corners of her eyes, to the edge of her nose.

As she looked back up, she and Sarah locked eyes. And they both understood.

Sixty-Seven

"Well, that was a nice temple, wasn't it?" Henry asked. He couldn't bear the tension any longer.

His parents didn't respond. They were doing a lot of that lately—not speaking—and Henry couldn't stand it. What a difference a few months could make. It used to be that Henry hated it when his parents spoke to him. Always questioning him, always judging. But now things were different. Now that Henry felt sure of himself, knew where he was going, he actually wanted to speak to his parents.

"The stained glass was really beautiful, I thought," Henry said, another attempt at discussion.

"It was," Ursella said. She was staring out the window, watching the world go by, barely paying attention.

"It was wonderful of the Golds to include us in the holiday this year," Edmond said. He was doing something he didn't do often—driving his own car—because with the changes at the bank (that's what Edmond and Ursella called them: changes), the Rothschild family was cutting back on expenses. They hadn't sold the house. They weren't facing total austerity just yet. But things that they'd taken for granted before—a driver, a chef—had been done away with.

Henry thought it was odd that his parents hadn't sold the house in Nice yet. He'd figured that would be the first thing to go. But maybe if things got too heated in New York, that could be a good place to hide out. Though, he would think that Morocco would be a smarter move. No extradition treaty.

"It was," Henry agreed. "I'm glad we were free this year."

"So are we, darling," Ursella said. "I just couldn't bear the thought of seeing all those people."

Henry knew that it was the thing both his parents were thinking—they didn't want to see anyone connected to their old life in Manhattan—but he wasn't expecting for her to say it quite so bluntly. In his experience, his parents didn't often say exactly what they were thinking.

"Well, I, for one, really like *these* people a lot more than *those* people anyway," Henry said.

Henry could see, in the rearview mirror, the edges of his father's mouth turn up ever so slightly.

Sixty-Eight

First, it had been the board from her museum committee. Wasn't it time, they asked, to give some of the younger volunteers a chance to plan their most high-profile fund-raising event? Ursella didn't know what to say. She'd been on the museum board since Edmond's mother was still alive. Three of the most important pieces from her art collection were on loan to the museum at that very moment, including the Rothschild egg, a Fabergé egg designed as a wedding gift for Edmond's great-aunt in 1902. Her name was on a brass plaque at the entrance to the sculpture garden. But now they didn't want it on the invitation.

Then, there was the Beatrice Club. The Rothschilds had been members since before Henry was even born. They'd spent countless holidays in the dining room, Henry had gone on the annual ski trips to St. Moritz throughout his childhood, and he'd even had his first kiss in the coatroom on the second floor during a particularly tedious Super Bowl party. They weren't kicked out of the club. The Beatrice Club wouldn't ever kick out one of its esteemed members (especially after cashing the enormous membership checks each year), but it was suggested to Edmond that his presence at this year's Rosh Hashanah dinner might make the other members uncomfortable. Perhaps he'd be interested in private dining in one of the conference rooms? Edmond was not.

The last straw was when Ursella went shopping for a new suit to wear to temple for the holiday. Ursella made an appointment, like she always did, with her personal shopper at St. John. She was so happy to be there. To escape the news. Escape her life for an hour. All she had to do was look at beautiful clothing and decide on an outfit. There was something about shopping that always made Ursella giddy. Growing up, she'd had no money, no options. Clothing had consisted of hand-me-downs from her siblings. It wasn't something to be enjoyed. It was only when she started dancing that she began to appreciate different fabrics, the way different colors changed her appearance, and how the right outfit could make her feel like another person altogether. It wasn't an entirely unwelcome feeling.

She browsed the store and picked out a few things to try on. Her personal shopper set her up in a fitting room with a bottle of seltzer water to sip while she made her choice. Ursella sat down on the tiny ottoman and flipped her shoes off. She looked at herself for a moment, clad only in a slip, and noticed how the stress of the past few months had taken its toll. Her face looked drawn, her cheeks sallow, and her skin had lost some of its luster.

Ursella tried the first suit on. It was a piqué knit, her favorite, in a rich red. Red always complemented her light-blond hair and pale skin. She spun around to inspect herself from every angle. She liked what she saw. The color red also reminded her of something her costume designer told her when she first joined the ballet—that it would ward off the evil eye. Those who were jealous of her wouldn't be able to wish ill on her if she wore red.

Ursella wore red often in those days. She knew that other girls like her, girls who wanted to get out just as madly as Ursella had, would be wishing her bad. They wouldn't see Ursella as an example. They would see her as someone who'd stolen their spot.

Ursella thought it might not be a bad idea to wear red for the High Holy Days this year. The evil eye, indeed. She would do anything to try to protect herself.

She took the suit off and carefully put it back on its hanger. She put her clothing back on. She didn't even need to try on the other suits—this red suit was the one. She unlocked the fitting room door and heard familiar voices—two of her friends from the museum committee.

"I doubt they'll show their faces this year," one said. "If you were Ursella, wouldn't you just shrivel up and die?"

The other one laughed a throaty laugh. As if she were not only enjoying the conversation, but enjoying the reversal of fortune the Rothschilds now faced. "But she's a ballerina, as Edmond likes to remind us all, so she would shrivel up and die very gracefully."

"Marilyn!" the first one chastised. "You're so bad."

"Do you have any idea how much money Phillip has lost over this?"

"Yes," the first one said. "We've lost a bundle, too. I'd like for them to just go away as well."

"I wish she were one of those ballerinas in a child's jewelry box. I wish I could just slam the box shut and never have to see her again."

"Let's toast to that!" Ursella could hear the salesperson

opening a bottle of champagne for the ladies. "To the Rothschilds leaving the island of Manhattan!"

Ursella sat down on the ottoman. How could she leave the
fitting room?

She heard hushed voices. Then a gasp. "I had no idea," one
said.

"Oh, I'm so embarrassed," the other said back.

"No, you're not." Then, they both laughed.

Ursella looked at her reflection in the mirror. She smoothed
her hair back with her hand. She reapplied her lipstick and then
walked out of the dressing room.

"Hello, ladies," she said with a smile. Then she walked to the
cash register to pay for her suit.

She'd escaped communist Russia by way of the goddamned
ballet. There was no way she was going to allow two Upper East
Side matrons, women who'd had their lives handed to them on a
platter, make her feel small.

Sixty-Nine

This time Sylvia was doing things differently.

She invited everyone back to the house after temple. Traditionally, she'd done a large holiday dinner the night before the holiday began, but she didn't feel up to it this year. This year, she was too tired. This year, she had other things occupying her mind.

She didn't scurry about the house, looking for areas in need of improvement. She didn't hire a chef or buy new linens. She set the table the night before, and didn't make seating arrangements. The guests would have to fend for themselves when it came to figuring out where they would sit. Cell phones would be allowed, copious glasses of wine would be served, and everyone would eat whenever they pleased.

The day before, she'd made her famous beef brisket. The one with the fresh crushed tomatoes and pressed garlic. The kitchen smelled like holiday. When she got back from temple, the ovens went on, and in went the brisket (always more delicious the second day), the tray of broccoli (simply prepared with garlic, salt, and pepper), and the oven-baked potatoes (the secret was the truffle oil). She got the matzoh ball soup into a pot to reheat, and then turned to the apples.

Sylvia heard the doorbell ring—everyone was beginning to shuffle in from temple—but she remained in the kitchen. She used to pre-cut the apple slices, using a squeeze of lemon to stave off the brown spots, but this time she decided to cut the apples just as her guests were arriving.

"Do you need some help in here?"

Sylvia looked up from the honey she was pouring into a pot. It was Sarah.

"Sure," Sylvia said. "I've got the gefilte fish already on plates in the fridge in the garage. Do you want to bring those out to the table? I bet people are hungry."

"No problem," Sarah said.

Sylvia lost herself in the slicing. She heard the family out in the living room, but she was happy right where she was. There was something therapeutic about the kitchen. Concentrating on one thing—slicing the apples into perfect little spheres—freed her mind. She was able to stop the constant torrent of thoughts that usually clouded her brain. It was just about the apple slices. And the lemon. She tried to find the perfect combination. Just a dash of lemon was needed to keep the apples from browning. Too much would alter the taste of the apples.

"All set," Sarah said, coming back into the kitchen. "Do you want me to pour you something to drink?"

"No, I'm fine," Sylvia said. "Do you want to see if everyone's ready to eat?"

"Dad's pouring wine," Sarah said. "So far, that's all people seem to want. And their apples. We're all ready for the apples."

Sylvia placed the apple slices on a tray. Then she took the pot of honey and put it squarely in the center.

"Why don't you go serve these to everyone." Sylvia said.

"Okay, but let's you and I have one first."

Sarah took an apple slice and dipped it into the honey. She handed it to her mother and then made one for herself.

"Happy New Year," Sarah said.

"To a sweet New Year," her mother replied.

Sarah grabbed the tray and walked toward the living room, but Sylvia realized something was missing.

"What?" Sarah asked.

"You need napkins," Sylvia said. She handed her the linen napkins. The embroidered ones, the ones with tiny little apples that Sarah had bought for her. Sarah could see that they had been laundered and ironed. They were crisp and clean and smelled faintly of her mother's special lavender laundry detergent. The one she reserved solely for her most special things.

Sarah nodded as she grabbed the napkins. And then she headed out to serve the apples and honey.

"What is that smell?" Valentina asked as she walked into the kitchen.

"You didn't have your apples and honey," Sylvia said. True, Sylvia wanted all of her guests to eat apples and honey to ensure a sweet New Year, but she was also stalling. She wasn't quite used to Valentina yet, and she had no idea how to interpret the question: What's that smell?

"I had one," Valentina said. "Gooey. Now, where are your forks?"

Sylvia pointed to her cutlery drawer and Valentina walked over and grabbed a fork. *The nerve of this woman.* Sylvia laughed to herself. And then: *At least she feels at home in my house.*

Valentina opened the oven door and found what she was looking for. She peeled back the aluminum foil and stuck the fork into the pan. The broken slice of brisket was piping hot—Sylvia could see the tiny puff of smoke from across the kitchen—so Valentina blew on it carefully and took a bite.

"Oh, this is good," she said, still chewing the meat. "Sarah's always carrying on about your brisket, and now I know why. I need the recipe for this."

"Of course," Sylvia said, pleased. Cooking was the one thing that Sylvia knew she was good at, but it was still always nice to hear the compliments. "Do you have a brisket recipe?"

"I do," Valentina said. "But I call it pot roast. I don't use a tomato-based sauce. I use a white wine and mushroom–based recipe."

"I'd like to try that," Sylvia said. And it surprised her to know that she was speaking the truth. She really did want to try it.

"You know, I feel like I have to apologize," Valentina said.

"I'm flattered that you like my cooking," Sylvia said, and Valentina furrowed her brow. Sylvia thought she was talking about sticking a fork into her food before she'd served it, but that's not why Valentina was apologizing.

"I mean about the kids," Valentina explained. "You know, at the time, I didn't think it was right what they did. Getting married without telling you. I really didn't think it was right. And I told them that. I want you to know that I told them that. But they were really intent on getting married, and I just love having your Sarah as a part of our family—you know, I always wanted a girl, did I ever tell you that?—and so there wasn't really anything I could do to change their minds."

"I appreciate that, Valentina," Sylvia said.

"I know you're mad at Sarah, and if I were you, I would be, too. I'd beat the living daylights out of Joey if he did that to me. But I just think you're so classy how you're being so quiet about the whole thing. And super gracious for having us all over like this."

"Alan and I are glad you're here."

"Thank you," she said. "Dominic's not too pleased with this whole conversion thing, but he'll come around. He's a good guy. I promise you that."

"He seems like a good man," Sylvia said. "And Joe hasn't decided whether or not he's converting, so you can tell Dominic, he needn't worry. In fact, I'm not sure that he will. I think he's enjoying learning. But nothing more."

"You try telling him that." Valentina laughed. "Maybe if you say it, he'll calm down."

"Well, if Joe does decide to convert, we can have his Bar Mitzvah party here in the backyard. I always wanted to throw a party with a tent in our backyard." Sylvia was joking, of course, but Valentina looked confused.

"A Bar Mitzvah?" Valentina asked. "Is that the one where they cut the boys' peenies off?"

"Um, no," Sylvia said, trying not to laugh at Valentina. "That's called a bris."

"Oh, okay," Valentina said. "That's what they do when the boys turn thirteen?"

"No," Sylvia said. Now she couldn't contain her laughter. "Jews don't circumcise their boys at age thirteen. It's done right after birth, just like everyone else does."

"Oh, right," Valentina said. "I knew that."

"Should we go eat?" Sylvia said and Valentina agreed that yes, it was time to eat.

Seventy

"Look at us: women in the kitchen, men out in the dining room, waiting to be served," Becca said and Sarah and their mother laughed.

"Joe offered to help," Sarah said.

"But then how could we talk about everyone if anyone else offers to help?" Sylvia said.

"How indeed," Sarah said.

Sylvia relayed the story to the girls, in fast whispers, of how Valentina thought that she was offering to host an adult bris for Joe, when she'd really been joking about an adult Bar Mitzvah.

"So, that's why people hate Jews," Becca surmised. "They think we want to chop off their peenies."

"I think Valentina understands that a bris is a circumcision, and not a castration," Sarah said.

"When did you stop being fun?" Becca asked, throwing an oven-roasted potato at her sister. "We're just joking around, you know."

"I'm still fun," Sarah said. She didn't realize it, but she was pouting.

"May I help?" Ursella asked. Sarah couldn't help but notice

how out of place Ursella looked in a kitchen. For starters, her outfit was all wrong. She wore a cherry-red knit suit, the sort of thing that just invited drips of sauce to come and take up residence in its creases. Then, there were her shoes. She wore impossibly high heels. Sarah had no idea how she could balance herself, much less two bowls of soup, perched so high.

"If you could bring these challahs to the table, that would be wonderful," Sylvia said.

"I'll help you with those," Becca said, taking one plate from Ursella.

"What can I do?" Sarah asked Sylvia.

"Just keep me company while I pour the soup into the bowls," Sylvia said.

Sarah remembered that that was her job when she was young—to watch her mother pour while she kept her company. When she was little, Sylvia was always afraid of the hot soup spilling on one of her kids, so she never let them near the pot, or even the bowls, as she served the soup. But they were allowed to sit at the kitchen counter and watch, to keep Sylvia company.

Valentina and Ursella came in, each taking turns bringing bowls of soup out to the dining room (Becca wasn't allowed— Sarah supposed she was still considered too young to handle hot soup), but Sarah remained. She stood by her mother's side as Sylvia prepared the bowls. When they were done, Sylvia turned to Sarah and said, "I'm sorry."

"No," Sarah said. "I'm sorry."

"I know, honey," her mother said. "Now, let's eat."

•   •   •

Sylvia served the main course as a buffet, and her guests heaped their plates high with her home cooking. She beamed with pride when her guests, one by one, went back for seconds. And then thirds.

"If you don't mind my saying," Edmond said, "I think your food is far superior to Chef Michael's. If I were you, I'd never hire a chef again."

"Thank you, Edmond."

"Yes," Ursella agreed. "Everything is delicious. Thank you for having us."

"My pleasure," Sylvia said.

"I'd like to make a toast," Alan said.

"You never make toasts," Sarah said under her breath, and Joe playfully grabbed her leg. "He doesn't," she whispered to him.

"To family," Alan said.

"To family," the crowd said back.

Sarah thought about saying more, about making her own toast about family. But then she looked around the table, at her sister, happy and in love; at her husband and his parents, finally sharing a meal with her family; and her parents, looking at each other from across the table, still in love, still connected after so many years of marriage. She decided that the moment didn't need another toast.

Sarah took a sip of wine, and then did something she would never normally do: she let go.

Acknowledgments

Thank you to my amazingly talented agent, Mollie Glick, who believed in me way back when. I'm so incredibly lucky to have you on my side. And to the fabulous Joy Fowlkes, who always has time for me, an ear for me—thank you. I just adore you two.

To my wonderful editor, Brenda Copeland: you really pushed me to write the sort of book I've always wanted to write. How can I thank you enough? I may be a writer, but words fail me when it comes to telling you what you mean to me. And to Laura Chasen, thank you for always being there to help keep me on track!

I'm so impossibly happy to be at St. Martin's. Endless thanks go to Sally Richardson, Jennifer Enderlin, George Witte, Jessica Katz, and Olga Grlic.

Thank you to my incredible publicists. Katie Bassel, you know exactly what to say and how to say it. Kathleen Zrelak, the word *no* isn't in your vocabulary; you take every crazy idea, every whim, and then, somehow, make it work. Katie and Kathleen, I'm so thrilled to have you two on my team—it's been a joy working with you.

Special thanks go to my parents, Bernard and Sherry Janowitz: my cheerleaders, my support system, my rocks. And thank you to the rest of my all-star family, too: Judy Luxenberg,

Jen and Lee Mattes, Stacey and Jon Faber, Stephanie and Sammy Janowitz.

My first-person essay angels: Susan Shapiro, Lynn Messina, Rachel McRady, and Anne Trubek. Thank you for reading. And reading. And reading. And giving amazing feedback. And then reading some more.

I've been so lucky to work with many amazing editors on my first-person essays: Tara Block, Adrienne Crezo, KJ Dell'Antonia, Rebecca Gruber, Olivia Hall, Cerentha Harris, the team at Hello Giggles, Sarah Hepola, Madeline Holler, Debbi Honorof, Amy Joyce, Brian Klems, Angelica Lai, Tyler Moss, Allison Slater Tate, and Jessica Strawser. Thank you for publishing my work— you are all responsible for so much of my joy over the past year.

Every writer needs good friends who will read countless drafts. Shawn Morris, Jennifer Moss, Danielle Schmelkin, and Tandy O'Donoghue: thank you.

My wonderful writer friends who have been a constant source of support, encouragement, and advice throughout the years: Jamie Brenner, Julie Buxbaum, Lynda Curnyn, Elyssa Friedland, Karin Gillespie, JP Habib, Kristin Harmel, Tracy Marx, Jason Pinter, Allison Winn Scotch, Melissa Senate, and Alex Sokoloff.

Special thanks to the incomparable Jennifer Weiner. You throw the best parties.

Endless thanks to my readers.

Finally, the biggest thank-you goes out to my husband, Douglas Luxenberg. Always the biggest and best to my husband. You are the love of my life, the father every child wants to have, and my best friend. Without you, none of this would be possible.

And to my children, Ben and Davey. I love you infinity times infinity.

1. Family holidays provide lots of dramatic fodder. Of all the holidays in a year, why do you think the author chose to set this novel around the holiday of Passover?

2. The title of the novel is *The Dinner Party*. What does this title mean to you? How does it work around the central premise of the book?

3. When Sarah discovers that her mother has hired a chef to cook their holiday meal, she is disappointed. What is the significance of food and Sylvia's decision to hire a chef for the seder? What is the significance of the food she cooks herself at Rosh Hashanah?

4. When Sylvia learns that the Rothschild family will be attending her seder, she undertakes an overhaul of her house. But Sylvia is the wife of a renowned doctor and lives in a lovely home in an affluent area. What made her so eager to please the Rothschilds? Have you ever tried to change your appearance to fit in with a group of people?

5. Sylvia's children all have biblical names. What do you think is the significance of the names Sarah and Rebecca, in terms of this story? Gideon?

6. Do you think that Sylvia truly forgave Sarah? Do you think that Sarah truly forgave Sylvia? When it comes to family, does forgiveness matter?

7. Do you think that Becca and Henry stay together? Why or why not? Do you think Joe eventually decides to convert to Judaism? Why or why not?

Discussion Questions

St. Martin's
Griffin

8. Sylvia and Valentina have a lot in common, even though they don't realize it. Do you think that Sylvia and Valentina will become friends?

9. In chapter eight, Sylvia says: "Life is harder for a woman." Do you think that is true? How so? Has anything changed from the time that Sylvia was young until now, when her daughters are young?

10. Valentina dotes on her only son. Did your opinion of her change when you learned that she was unable to have more children?

11. In chapter thirty-five, Sylvia talks to Gideon about the importance of Jews marrying Jews. Do you think it's important to marry within your faith? Why or why not?

12. What do you think is the message of the book? Is there a scene or a passage that articulated the theme of the book to you?